Seducing Mr. Right

Seducing Mr. Right

REBECCA ROSE

FOREVER YOURS

New York Boston

Copyright © 2014 by Rebecca Rose
Excerpt from *Tempting Mr. Perfect* copyright © 2014 by Rebecca Rose
Cover design by Elizabeth Turner
Cover image © Juhasz Peter / Getty Images
Cover copyright © 2014 by Hachette Book Group, Inc.

Forever Yours
Hachette Book Group
237 Park Avenue
New York, NY 10017
hachettebookgroup.com
twitter.com/foreverromance

First published as an ebook and as a print on demand: April 2014

Forever Yours is an imprint of Grand Central Publishing.
The Forever Yours name and logo are trademarks of Hachette Book Group, Inc.

The publisher is not responsible for websites (or their content) that are not owned by the publisher.

The Hachette Speakers Bureau provides a wide range of authors for speaking events. To find out more, go to www.hachettespeakersbureau.com or call (866) 376-6591.

ISBN: 978-1-4555-7789-7 (ebook edition)
ISBN: 978-1-4555-8142-9 (print on demand edition)

I'd like to dedicate this story to my dad,
Army Specialist Roger J. Roy. He's no longer
with us but was a huge supporter of my writing career.
I love you, Dad. The kids and I miss our Pépère every day.

I'd also like to thank every soldier who's fought,
or is fighting, to preserve freedom at the cost of losing
everything they love. I stand in awe of your bravery.

Acknowledgments

This story took me two years to write and research. I needed to get all my information correct as to honor the men and women who have served or are serving. My uncle, Tank and Armor Command Equipment Specialist and Sergeant First Class Bernard Bolduc; his wife, Shirley Bolduc; and my stepfather, First Sergeant Scott Ryer, assisted me with the scenes that were too emotional and too complicated for a civilian to understand. They were patient with my many questions, believed in me enough to open up about their time in combat, and then were candid about recovery. This is a gift given to very few, and to them I say thank you with all my heart.

Chapter 1

The first step and the hardest step are often one and the same. Sophie repeated this pep talk while her insides shook and her stomach turned ripe with bile. She was ready for this change and had been working toward it despite everyone's objections and her own apprehension. After all, Greenwich, Connecticut, was a long way from the outskirts of Boston, and many of the socialites in her parent's circle believed only a lower class of people worked in bars.

"This is the bar. Obviously." Sophie's new boss, Dave, turned and grinned at her. "We open at two and close at one-thirty Thursday, Friday, and Saturday. Two to ten every other night. We serve small meals, typical bar food stuff."

Sophie listened as the man before her went down the list of what her manager job would entail at the Hungry Lion Bar-n-Grill. Excitement bubbled inside her as nerves danced beneath her skin. Deep in thought about what she could bring to her new position, she ran her hand along the silky wheat-colored bar counter. The sun streamed in through the stained-glass window, which portrayed a fierce lion battling a man with a sharpened stick. The walls were a light tan and the stool covers and booth seats bloodred. Her heels clicked on the scarred, wood-paneled floors as she walked to the back.

"And this is the office." Dave opened a door and nodded for her to enter.

At first, nothing seemed unusual. The walls were mostly bare and a drab blue. Under the only tiny window in the room sat her desk with multiple piles of papers laying in wait. Everything was clean and—Sophie stopped abruptly at the sound of snoring to her left.

"Lord's sake!" Dave yelled. He turned and gave an apologetic smile to Sophie. "My baby brother, Jake." Dave lifted a booted foot and pushed on the sleeping man's bare back. "Jake! Where the hell are your clothes?"

Feeling a little flushed, Sophie examined the slumbering man. Jake was covered only by his boxers, and his muscular back and legs were left bare for her hum of approval. A harsh scar—*that must have been a nasty wound*—stretched down his left side, while a cleaner, surgical one ran just below it. When he shifted and threw an arm over his head, Sophie took an appreciative glance at the tree-trunk arms peppered with pockmarks.

"Jake."

Jake made an inaudible noise and burrowed deeper into the cushions.

"Don't disturb him on my account. We can work around him."

"Well, I don't think we'll be able to move him, anyway. Damn kid. Must have been celebratin' pretty hard last night to stay here. He's got a key to let himself in since he's been helpin' with the books. As much as I'd like to tell you this doesn't happen, it does from time to time. I was just hopin' you wouldn't find out until you were here for a while. This doesn't change your mind about the job, does it?"

Sophie looked at the mostly nude man sleeping on her office couch. If she wanted this job, then she was going to have to get used to the ways of the bar-n-grill scene. "Oh, I don't know, Dave. Coming into work every now and then and finding a naked man on my couch doesn't seem like such a hardship."

Dave laughed and gave Jake another hardy push with his foot. "At least you have a sense of humor about this. Okay, let me get the computer booted up and I'll show you what we've screwed up."

"You're screwing up my sleep, right now," the strained voice from the couch announced.

"Where the hell are your clothes, Jake?"

"I don't know, but I'm cold."

After much effort to suppress it, Sophie let out a good-natured snort. "Sorry," she told Dave.

"Not your fault." Dave grabbed a threadbare blanket from the office closet and covered Jake's massive body. "You'd never know we were brothers. This man works out like it's his job."

Sophie really tried to look disapprovingly at Jake but knew she didn't quite pull it off. The few men of her past never had physiques like that, and they each tended to have more of a feminine build.

"And that. That sparkle in your eye," Dave said, while pointing a finger at her, "is why he does it."

She glanced down at the sleeping man, now covered up by an afghan. She desperately wanted to uncover him but didn't dare. So instead, Sophie relived the memory of his strong naked torso and legs. She would definitely have a little fantasy about him later. After all, Sophie was a woman who appreciated a good-looking man.

Two long hours later, after sorting through old paperwork and files on an even older computer, Sophie realized they were in a bigger mess than Dave had let on. Maybe this job was exactly where she was supposed to be. Promotional ideas popped into her head for how to create more income and spend less—problems the Hungry Lion seemed to be having.

She eyed the sleeping figure across from her. They could always host a woman's night with male dancers. A sly smile crept across her face. Maybe Jake could make up this terrible first impression by hosting it...or dancing in it. Who knew, maybe it was one of his side jobs. *With a body like that, he must be doing something that requires plenty of strength.*

As if on cue, Jake rolled over and off the couch. He landed with a loud thud and grunt. Sophie sprinted out of her dilapidated office chair and to his side.

"Are you okay?"

Jake looked at her with red-rimmed eyes. She could see him trying to focus on her face and not quite getting the control he needed. "Who are you?"

"The new manager. Are you all right?"

"Yeah." Jake brought his knees up to his chest and rested his head on them.

Feeling the need to soothe the giant, Sophie petted Jake's curling brown hair. It was shoulder length and in bad need of a cut. "Jake," she whispered.

"I think I'm going to be sick."

Sophie snatched her wastebasket. "Here."

"Jesus. Where are my clothes?" At her chuckle he turned to her. "This is not funny."

"Oh, it absolutely is. Your clothes are on the side table."

"How did I..." His eyes rolled a little, and Sophie put an arm around the massive man to keep him from falling over.

"This is what I want you to do. I went out and got you some Gatorade and you need to drink it. You're probably dehydrated, and that's making you even sicker than whatever it is you drank."

"Maybe I don't want to."

"Maybe you don't have a choice."

"Okay."

He sounded pathetic and Sophie couldn't help chuckling. She grabbed the bottle and gave it to him with the cap off. The container looked unbelievably small in his hands, and a flash of what it would be like to have them on her caused a heated blush to rise to her cheeks.

"Let's get you back on the couch." He moaned when she put his arm over her shoulder. "Now, you need to help me Jake, you're a big boy and I'm a small girl." *Who would love to be under you, over you, wherever it is you'd like me to be positioned.* She gave a small giggle at her perverse thoughts. If Jake was one of the perks to working at the Lion, she was really going to enjoy her new job.

* * *

Jake woke a few hours later. The bugles in his head were finally silenced, and the drums had ceased to play. But Jake felt as if they had been replaced by the vice now squeezing his skull. At least he'd slept, even if it hadn't been a fully restful slumber. He didn't wake up soaked in sweat from fighting imaginary demons trying to kill him.

He rolled to a sitting position and sniffed. The cook seemed to be making something greasy. The delicious smell of cooking oil filled his senses, and Jake briefly wondered if his new recipe was being tried out. At least his stomach didn't turn and lurch at the aroma. He would take that as a good sign.

Bit by bit, Jake scanned the old storage room that became their office. Something was different, and he couldn't quite put his finger on it. But then again, he wasn't really in the right frame of mind to be concentrating on anything. His brain began to clear, and the distant memory of a lady's voice broke through the fog. She had helped him drink the power drink and given him a damp cloth on the back of his neck when he heaved in what he assumed was the wastebasket next to him. The embarrassment of someone taking care of him caused nausea, once again, to threaten the reversal of his already empty stomach. Jake was a military man—he took care of people, not the other way around. With one hand holding his head and the other reaching for his pants, Jake heard the door open.

"Good. You're up."

He couldn't see who owned the sweet voice, but he knew it belonged to the woman who'd nursed him earlier. Slowly, he turned his head to look at her but she was out of his line of sight. Resigned to the fact that he was only in boxers and didn't remember how he had been stripped down, Jake tried to pull on his pants.

"Oh, dear. Here, let me help you."

Jake looked into his rescuer's soft blue eyes and small freckled nose. The primal male in him wanted to see the rest of her, but the miserable head on his shoulders wouldn't allow it. She smiled and helped him to put one foot in his jeans and then the next. With a little aid, Jake stood and she pulled them up.

"I think you can take it from here."

"You're not going to zip them for me?"

She scoffed at him. "And miss you struggling? No."

He watched her walk around the steel desk and sit. "That's my desk." At her questioning brow, Jake elaborated, "I keep the books for my brother."

"So I have you to thank for this mess?"

"Mess? No, they were like that when I got them. Where are my paper piles?"

"Organized." She smirked.

He brought a hand to his head then sat back down. "Shit. What the hell happened last night?"

"That's the million-dollar question in the bar right now. Apparently you came back here with Trixie."

"Trixie? Do I know a Trixie?"

"Well if you didn't, you do now."

"I'm sorry. Who are you?" At the knock on the door Jake moaned and the woman in front of him got up to answer it.

"Thanks, Dave. No, you can't come in."

Jake heard his brother grunt, "I don't see why not."

"Because you can harass him once he's off my couch. But right now I want him in a good mood in case he plans to camp out in here any longer."

"I'm not camping out," Jake grumbled. "And who the hell are you?" He watched her bump the door shut with her hip as she balanced a bowl of soup in one hand and a sandwich on a plate in the other. There was something graceful and precise about the way she did it.

"I'm the new manager. Dave told me to tell you, 'You know, the one I told you about yesterday before I left.'"

Jake cringed. "I'm such an idiot. Sorry. If my head would just roll off I could get out of your hair."

"Here, eat this. It's chicken broth. Forget the sandwich."

Taking the bowl from her, Jake looked at the woman before him. She had light brown hair, very tiny hands, and red glossed lips. He licked his own in response to staring at them. He supposed she must have seen him doing it, because she shifted on her feet and moved back behind the desk.

"Eat," she urged him.

"Thank you...Umm, I still don't know your name."

"Sophia."

"Just Sophia?" It amused him to see her roll those large doll-like eyes.

"Sophia Agnés. They call me Sophie. And, you are?"

"Jake Sanders."

"Jake?"

"Yeah?"

"Eat your broth or it's going to get cold."

He saw it. The quick flick of the eye when it shifts to see something clearer and then moves back just as fast. Her gaze had gone to his chest. Uneasy, Jake tried to remember the last time a woman had looked at him bare-chested. Sophie sat with her hands folded in front of her watching him, clearly trying not to notice he was still half-undressed and scarred. Suddenly it felt like that dream where he was giving an oral report in high school, only to look down and notice the only thing he had on was his underwear. A strange feeling, seeing that up until a little while ago, that *was* all he had on.

Jake put the soup down on top of a small filing cabinet then gave her a weak smile. "I'm chilly." He bent and picked up his shirt then slid it over his head. "Thanks for mothering me. Not much of a first day, eh?"

"You're forgiven. Now at the risk of sounding rude...I need to get back to reviewing your revenue. Or lack thereof." The look on her face told Jake of the hopelessness she felt toward balancing the books, then she started clicking keys again.

"If you need any help, just give a holler. Actually, please whisper today." He discovered he liked making her smile. It brightened up her face and showed in her eyes. Jake hoisted himself off the couch and picked up his bowl of soup. As much as he would have liked to stay and make her flash that grin again, he knew he should get out of the way so Sophie could work. Besides, he probably smelled as bad as he felt.

"I wouldn't go out there, if I were you." He turned and saw she never looked up from her computer. "Stay. At least you'll have peace and quiet. They're planning on razzing the living hell out of you, and I don't think you can take it yet."

"Why do you think that?"

"Because you're still green."

He laughed because she was right. He felt a little green and besides...looking at a lovely lady sitting behind a desk wasn't such a hardship. "Would it bother you if I went back to sleep?"

"Only if you don't eat the soup first."

* * *

The day went by quicker than Sophie thought possible. She made a mental note to bring in some small plants and pictures the next day to make her new office cozier. When Jake finally left for home to sleep off the remainder of his hangover, there'd been hoots and hollers from the patrons. Sophie felt kinda bad for the big guy. He'd only wanted to get out without being harassed, and he'd even contemplated trying to squeeze through the office window. Sophie had assured him there was no way he would fit.

Once home, she slipped on her pink fuzzy slippers and ran down the day's activities to her childhood friend, Kathy. The one person she could always count on and would always listen to.

"Sooooo, how's the new job?"

"Good." Sophie took a bite of her lasagna while cradling the phone to her ear. "Dave, my boss, is pretty cute."

"Really? Tell me more."

"He's tall, dark, and handsome."

Kathy made a gagging noise. "Really? You can't come up with anything better than that?"

"Okay, okay. He's much more your type than mine. Dave is supernice, very considerate, and has nice lips. His brother has a great body," she added under her breath.

"What? What! Speak louder, girl."

"Dave's brother, Jake, was passed out on my office couch for most of the day, and half-naked. Kathy, I don't think I've ever seen a man with a body like his before. I mean he turned me on just by lying there."

Kathy giggled into the phone. "Yum. What do you plan on doing with this hunky brother?"

"Nothing. I wouldn't know what to do with a man like that, and I'm terrible at flirting."

"Oh, come on! Have a little fun. Plus, your parents aren't here to reprimand you, so go wild."

"He looks like trouble."

"Even better."

Sophie gave out a loud huff. "I'll tell you what. If I change my mind and decide to start a little something with a man who can make you sweat with just a glance at his arms, you'll be the first to know and my mother the last."

"Promise?"

Sophie let the cloak of doubt guide her next words: "I don't know, Kathy. Maybe it's too soon."

"Hmmm...maybe you're chickenshit."

"Could be that, too."

Chapter 2

Yes Mom, I'm fine... Yes, I know I don't usually drink like that... No, I'm not going to do it again anytime soon. Yesterday was just..." Jake walked into the Hungry Lion and saluted the patrons and Dave. They all called back to him in return. "There's no need to worry, I'm fine."

"Is your mommy on the phone givin' poor Jakie a hard time?" Louie teased.

"I guess the boy can't hold his liquor anymore," Stuart hollered from his barstool perch.

Jake flipped them all off. "Yes, I love you too, Ma."

He closed his cell phone and glared at the older patrons sitting at the bar. Louie smiled and said, "Did you find out who Trixie is yet, Gunny?"

"I heard she's a real looker," Stuart taunted.

Louie picked his beer up and pretended to examine the contents, "I heard he made a damn fool out of himself by throwing up on her, too," he snickered.

Jake moved like a panther, his well-toned body quick and agile. Louie, his prey, sprinted around the bar as Jake moved in pursuit. One of Jake's massive hands clutched the other guy's arm and brought him down to the ground in good-humored fun. They knocked over a chair and table as they wrestled, and Jake could hear his brother yelling but didn't pay any bother. Not until a shooting pain came from his ear. Jake instantly realized those eleven years as a Marine, most of which were on the front line, was no match for a woman with two fingers twisting his ear, and him, into submission. Disbelief carried embarrassment to the front of his thoughts and Jake had to push down the apology it left on the tip of his tongue. The woman standing over him looked spitting mad and devilishly sensual.

"I win," Sophie announced. When Louie laughed she stared him down with one fierce look. Both men went quiet along with all the customers. Jake looked her up and down with an admiring smirk. There was something perversely attractive about Sophie not being a pushover.

"Get your ass off the floor. And you…" She turned to Jake and pointed. Before he could stop himself, his feet took two steps back. "Clean up this mess. Then I need you in the office." Jake watched her hips swing as she marched to the back. She was one hot chick.

"Damn, Jake. You really know how to impress the ladies." Dave wiped a mug dry with a dish towel. "Her first day she comes into her office with you passed out naked on the couch. You spend hours in there smelling like booze and vomit, then when she gets to meet you all cleaned up and lookin' decent as you can, she has to break up a fight."

"We weren't fighting." Jake picked up the table they knocked over. When it teetered on a broken leg he let out an agitated breath. His good mood quickly turned sour.

"Sure seems like you were fightin' by the looks of my table. How's the chair?"

Jake snarled at his brother, "I'll fix it."

"If I were you, I'd take those out back before she sees them, then get your butt in her office. That there woman is tough to be takin' you on." Every man in the bar voiced agreement with Dave. But instead of commenting like he wanted to, Jake picked up the small round table and motioned to his partner in crime to take the chair.

"Damn it. Having this place being run by a woman is the last thing we need. She'll probably have the joint wallpapered with flowers by Christmas." Jake placed the table upside down then turned to leave. His body came to an abrupt halt at the sight of Sophie. Even his heart skidded to a stop as his eyes took in the woman before him—dynamite in a pretty little inconspicuous package. A combination Jake loved in life and one he now avoided due to the damage they could cause.

"I was thinking of doing the bathroom only in flowers," Sophie told him. "Just the men's room, of course." Her arms were crossed at her chest, and for the first time Jake noticed Sophie's breasts. With her arms folded, they settled nicely on top and he had to tear his eyes from them.

"Look, Sophie. I'm sorry."

"I have to leave. I just thought I'd let you know. I already talked to Dave."

The unwavering irritation in her eyes pulled Jake to step to her instead of away. "Everything okay?"

"Yup. Just some unfinished moving."

At Sophie's clipped response, Jake followed her back into the office. "Wow. The place looks nice with some plants and stuff."

"Thanks."

He watched in fascination as she grabbed her purse and violently swung it over her shoulder. She was so naturally sexy in a wicked way. His hands itched to touch, his mouth to taste. He wasn't quite sure what to do with the unexpected attraction, so he got pushy. "What's going on?"

With a mildly irritated tone she told him, "None of your concern."

"Well, I think it is."

"You're not my boss," she said.

"I'm one of them. I own half of this." A smile tugged at his lip as he gestured to the building they were standing in.

"Look, Jake, I'm sure you're a great guy and all, but there are some things that are best not discussed."

"When you leave early on your second day—"

"Dave doesn't have a problem with this." Her voice rose slightly, and he respected the way she reined in her temper. The women of his past always seemed to prefer yelling and screaming. Sophie's careful breaths restrained her and gave him a wild thrill of what would happen if she let her temper go. Emotions ran through his body, unfamiliar and none too comfortable. The last few years he'd been trying to feel something. Anything. Anger, grief, joy. They all seemed to elude him, stolen the night of the ambush, until this very moment when Sophie challenged him to fight back. He checked the frustration he felt. She wasn't to blame for what he had lived through. But, she sure was testing his restraint, and he wanted information.

"Dave wouldn't. I do."

"Fine." Sophie's heels clicked as she walked to him with vengeance in her eyes. He wasn't certain, but he really thought for a minute she was going to clock him in the eye. Instead, she said, "My ex-fiancé needs me to come and pick up what's left in my ex-home because his pregnant girlfriend is moving in, in two days. See! Some things are better left unsaid."

"How long have the two of you been broken up?"

She tapped her foot impatiently on the floor.

"Just asking questions. Reasonable questions," he said, with his hands up in the air.

"Six months if you count the day I kicked his ass out."

"Wait. *You* kicked *him* out? Then how did he get the house?"

"It's our summer place. It never felt like a home anyway, so he's more than welcome to have it."

Jake cocked his head and looked at Sophie with a new respect for the strong, capable, and not-to-be-pushed-around woman. She amazed him.

"I was supposed to be able to go up this weekend and get the rest of my things, but he decided to go ahead of me and prepare the baby's room," she explained while shifting on her feet. It was the first bruised emotion she showed, and it told Jake Sophie was still carrying wounds from the breakup.

"I'm sorry." Jake put an understanding hand on her arm, hoping to comfort her as she had done for him the day before.

She batted his hand away. "Don't worry, Jake. I'm past the hurt. I don't even care if he didn't get all my stuff in boxes. That's not what this is about."

Puzzled, Jake looked deeper into her eyes. He saw there what he'd seen in many of his comrades—the look you get while preparing to go to war. A mind-set that the inevitable will happen. "You'd really like to punch his lights out."

"Yup. And I'm hoping he'll give me a reason to."

Jake leaned against the office door with a smirk and crossed his legs at the ankles. Fire built in her eyes at his obstructing her exit. He wondered what would send her into a blaze. "Yesterday when you were nursing me, I thought you were an angel."

"I was. If it was up to those guys out there, you would've had makeup on your face and your fingernails painted." She shifted. "I'd love to continue this conversation, but I really need to leave, Jake."

He laughed because she was so right on the truth. They would have done that and probably much more. "What about Trixie?" he asked her.

A shy smile formed on her lips while an impatient hand pulled her purse strap tighter on her shoulder.

Jake shook his head. "You knew there was no Trixie."

"You deserved it." She began to pace the room with jerky movements. "Your brother told you I was starting, and now you're trying to get me off the subject of my ex. Thanks, but I need to go. Move."

He didn't budge when she tried to get by him. Jake knew the need to get pent-up aggression out, so he let her shove him, smack his arms, and hiss vulgar threats. "Do you know how to ask?"

"Move, damn it!"

She became increasingly more volatile with slaps and swears while Jake used his hands to protect himself. "Sophie, I'm going to ask you nicely to stop." When she kicked him in the shin, Jake controlled himself from pushing her to the floor. "I understand you're upset and I don't mind you taking some of that out on me, but that hurt."

Sophie growled at him, "I wouldn't have to hurt you if you'd just move."

"You need to calm down—"

"I do not need to calm down. I need to leave." She tried kicking him again, but Jake dodged it.

"Wow, you're feisty. I'm going to ask you again to stop or I'll stop you."

"Yeah, right. Move, damn it!" She pushed at him with both

hands, but before she could get any more physical, Jake stopped her. He cuffed her wrists above her head with one hand and pinned her back against the door. The move left only mere inches between their vibrating bodies.

"Sophie, do you need help getting the stuff? Or maybe someone to come along and make sure you don't do anything stupid?" When her eyes narrowed at him, Jake repeated the questions.

"I can control my temper very well, and there is nothing heavy I need to get. Now let go of me."

Jake tilted his head to the side and examined her still body. Lust shot through his loins for the woman before him. In reflex, he moved a little closer. "You know most women would be frightened by me doing this to them."

"Don't even think about it, Jake."

The warning he saw in her eyes had him thinking twice about placing that hand on her rib cage and slowly moving it up to mold her breast. It had been so long since he'd felt the pull of a woman that the urge became almost uncontrollable. Almost. With little control left, Jake reminded himself that he really didn't need further complications in his life. Especially the female kind.

"Would you like me to go along and scare the crap out of him? I don't even have to do anything physical." He saw her processing the information so he added, "It would make up for yesterday. Plus, I won't have to worry about getting a call that you need bail money. That would ruin my day." Without thought, his eyes roamed her curvy body. By the way she held herself, he was certain she'd been a ballerina. Where she rested on her toes, they were pointed. Her body was stretched up farther then would be comfortable for someone without training, and she held her head with an unmistakable eloquence.

"Okay," she said with a husky tone. "Now will you please let me go?" When he did, she socked him in the gut with her right fist. Despite his toned abs, the air rushed out of Jake's mouth.

"What the hell was that for?"

"Today and that flower comment. Also, don't ever touch me like that again."

The seriousness in her face was real, and Jake found himself too shocked to say a word. Years of training in combat situations, and this woman planted a right hook to his gut that he never saw coming.

"Okay, Jake. Let's go." She picked up her purse and sashayed out of the office. Jake stood where he was for a moment processing the fact that a woman just got the best of him. In his disbelief he was struck dumb. Empty to all thought except, *Next time be more alert, and be thankful she's not the enemy.*

* * *

Her fist hurt but she would never admit to it. His harder-than-rock stomach nearly broke her hand. She flexed it while sitting in the passenger seat, hoping Jake wouldn't notice.

"Listen, Sophie. I'm sorry if I scared you earlier. I was just trying to protect myself."

"You didn't scare me…well, not that much." She gave him a weak smile. "Besides, I'd kick your ass."

"Seriously, I've never gotten violent with a woman unless she was trying to kill me."

When he grabbed her hand and gave it a little squeeze, Sophie realized Jake was truly serious. He actually looked revolted by the prospect that he might have frightened her.

"Thank you. But I never felt in danger. You know, we really could have taken my car," she said.

"Yup, and I can put my feet behind my head."

"It's not that small." She laughed when he gave her a quick bland stare. "The Prius is very comfortable and roomy. That's what the salesman told me."

"How tall are you? Five-seven? Five-eight? I'm just shy of six-three and almost as wide."

Sophie flicked the dice hanging from his rearview mirror. "Wow. We're not into ourselves, are we?"

"No. I'm just saying you put a man of my size in a car like that and it's not going to work."

Sophie enjoyed watching him scowl out the front windshield. He was so nice to look at when he wasn't hung over and stinky. His nose was slightly crooked. His skin was so white she thought there quite possibly might be some Swedish descent.

"Do you always drink like that? Dave said you crash on the couch fairly often." She pressed her lips together to stop grinning when he gave her a quick glance.

"No. I don't normally drink like that. And I was crashing there quite often because I didn't have a place of my own. There was an electrical fire in my building and I was out of power for a while. I have my own place now."

Sophie shifted in her seat to have a better view of him. "So, you're not the normal 'party animal boozing it up and taking swanky girls named Trixie into the office' kinda man?"

"*Ha!* I'm actually a pretty boring guy, and I prefer it that way."

"Fair enough." They fell into surprisingly comfortable silence as the highway stretched on. After all, she did have what looked to be the bodybuilder of the year sitting next to her; minus the bulging veins. Her libido began to work overtime, while her brain tried to calm it down.

"You're going to take the next exit and then make a left."

"This is a nice area off the Sound. I'm surprised you're willing to give it up."

"He's paying dearly for it." Sophie played with the dog tags hanging from the cigarette lighter. "Besides, it's where he took his other girlfriend when he was supposed to be on business trips."

"Ouch."

Sophie laughed at how blasé her own voice sounded. "I just don't care that much. I think of him as one of those slime bags you read and talk about with distaste because you can't help it. You'll understand when you meet him."

"And you didn't see this when you first met him? Oh wait, let me guess. He wasn't like that."

She took in Jake's profile. His strong jaw set in a grim scowl, his hands rigid on the steering wheel, and the actuality that he truly seemed to want to know what happened. "If you hold that wheel any tighter you're going to break it. From your reaction I'd say you don't like the helpless-female routine."

"What would make you say that? I'm all for equal rights, saving the heroine and yada yada yada."

"Well, the yada is code for, 'I had a girl that I loved and she was stuck on some jerk that didn't treat her right.'"

"How did this turn into a conversation about me? And she's now married to that jerk, thank you very much."

"But you could see yourself loving her?"

Jake took the left fast enough to have the tires on his truck squeal. Sophie's hands fisted the camouflage covers on his seats. "Whoo, hit a nerve. I'm sorry. I was only teasing."

"It's okay. So if you knew he was an asshole, why did you stay and agree to marry him?"

How could she explain this to someone who couldn't possibly understand? It was almost like puppy-dog love. She'd been so blind and had seen nothing until one day she realized the man of her dreams, the one whom her parents trusted and accepted despite their twelve-year age difference, was a womanizer only looking for the big prize—her parents' wallet. The fact that her mother and father were accepting with this truth was another sting. It was good business for her to marry him.

"He was my ballet instructor."

"I knew you were a dancer by the way you hold yourself!"

"Really? Dated a few?"

"One, actually," he said, while winking at her. "But her pirouetting was on a pole."

Sophie snorted. "Nice. Anyway, I was young when I met him and thought of him as a god. I put off marrying him until he finally threatened to leave me. Then we set a date for two years later."

"Not much for the marriage thing, eh?"

"Not much for ignoring my instincts, which got me into a lot of trouble in the dance world."

"Break a few noses?"

He was fun, and Sophie decided she liked him. "Someone broke yours." She gave him a playful punch to the arm.

"No person broke mine, sweetheart. It was flying debris from a car bomb that hit me smack in the face. Trust me when I say I was much prettier at one time."

"Oh, I have no complaints with how you look. You'll need to slow down, by the way. The driveway is up on the right."

The smell of the ocean broke her thoughts. She could hear it outside the car window. The salt hung heavy in the air, and so did her sigh. Some things never changed, and this was no different. Bruce was standing outside the lavish house waiting for her.

Chapter 3

Jake looked at the slender man standing on the front crescent-shaped stone steps. He wore fitted black pants with a crisp white shirt unbuttoned to his navel to expose his hairless chest. The red scarf resting around his neck fluttered in the ocean breeze while his hair stayed perfectly still from being heavily shellacked. His skin gleamed with a yellowish glow, which made Jake grimace at the thought of the man being so self-absorbed he used the tanning spray Jake once heard about.

"God, I hate this house. All three stories of it. Is it not the most pretentious thing you've ever seen?"

Jake parked the truck, and before Sophie could get out he took her hand and kissed her knuckles. "No, it isn't. *He* is."

"Really? Are you trying to be romantic with me?"

Jake winked. "No, I just wanted to tease your ex." Seeing the laughter in her eyes promised to make this much more enjoyable. He had a sneaky suspicion Sophie was the type of person who liked to harass the people she didn't like.

"Hey, asshole!" He heard her say while getting out of the truck. "Couldn't wait, could ya?"

Jake stifled a laugh then smiled when he heard the man's response.

"Sophia, my love, there is no need to be nasty."

"Oh, but I think there is."

Jake came to stand behind her then rested a protective hand on her shoulder. The negative energy coming off of her was enough to have Jake thinking of a strategy on how to get her out of there if things got out of hand. A fantasy flirted in his head of her doing something that would warrant him flinging her over his shoulder. The thought of Sophie being pressed so firmly against him made parts of Jake's body twitch.

"Jake this is Bruce. Bruce, Jake."

When Bruce extended a hand, Jake looked at it with distaste. "Where's her stuff?"

"Well, actually I wasn't expecting you to come with someone, honey. I wanted to talk to you."

"First, I'm not your honey, and second, we have nothing to talk about. Third, where's my stuff, Bruce?"

Jake stepped in front of Sophie; his body tensed as his protective soldier instincts switched on. He crossed his arms and took it as a good sign when Bruce looked nervously at him. Mission to intimidate was accomplished. A smile lifted the corners of his mouth.

"I'd really like to speak to you alone, Sophia." Bruce repeated while trying to look around Jake to see her.

He was stalling, and it became apparent Bruce had more on his mind then Sophie picking up her stuff. "Where's her stuff, *Bruce?*" Jake drew out his name while flexing his massive arms at the same time.

Bruce stepped away from Jake and took Sophie by the arm. "I don't want to talk in front of him."

"Well, that's too bad. What do you want?"

The impression of a wolf in sheep's clothing came to mind when Bruce looked at Jake and gave a shaky smile. "Jake, right?" When Jake nodded, Bruce continued, "I'm not sure of your relationship with Lady Sophia, but I can assure you she's not one to be tamed, and all this business with us was blown out of proportion. I don't believe you know her well enough to understand the world could be hers if she got her affairs in order."

Jake snickered. "You're a funny guy, Bruce." He glanced at Sophie, who stuck her tongue in her cheek and gave him a *go for it* nod. Admiration for her ability to stay calm filled him. "I was under the impression that you were the one who had the affairs."

Bruce dithered for a moment. "We're men here. You obviously respect the finer qualities of the body. You can't tell me that you don't have multiple prospects. As a human, I don't believe we are meant to be with one woman."

"Well…I can't speak for all men, but I can tell you that Trixie's been the only woman I've been around for a while. See, my family believes marriage is an oath two people take that's for the rest of their lives. I guess what I'm saying is, I don't understand your warped view of a relationship." Jake took a step forward and Bruce stepped back. "Where's her stuff?"

Bruce visibly swallowed. "In the garage. But I still want to talk to Sophia. I don't know where all this bitterness is coming from. I don't know what's gotten into you. You're so hostile lately. I'd really like a chance to make this up to you. We do so well together."

Sophie laughed and sauntered toward the four-car garage. "In your dreams, Bruce. And you can drop the greater-than-thou act. You sound ridiculous."

"You need me and you know it. You can't even go onstage without a pep talk. Who's going to do that for you? *This* guy?"

He thumbed toward Jake as they all briskly walked to the garage. "I have a feeling here, honey, that he's cheating you."

"What?" Sophie and Jake asked in unison.

"He's pulling you along while with this Trixie woman. What a preposterous name. It brings on visions of seedy motels and women of the night! Come on, listen to me, I know what's right for you."

Sophie's ability to look so blandly at Bruce, as if she really didn't care what he said because it was all bull, impressed Jake. He wanted to plant his fist in the man's face but, like a good sergeant, he knew he needed to wait for her signal. So he watched as she, with more effort than necessary, pressed the code in for the garage door to open. As the door slowly slid ajar, her laughing gaze settled on Jake's.

"You're having fun, aren't you?" Jake whispered in her ear.

"Maybe," she replied.

But before the two of them could walk inside, Bruce jumped in front of her. "Come back to me. I've been miserable for months now."

"Bruce, we broke up six months ago and your girlfriend is, what...eight months pregnant? Get out of my way." Sophie walked around him and through the open door. Jake moved fast to her side when her body came to a sudden halt. The garage was empty except for a Mercedes.

"Honey," Bruce hurried to explain, "I never thought you'd show up with someone, I—"

"You thought I'd come back to you." Sophie's fist rose and hit Bruce square in the eye. As Jake half-choked and half-laughed, she turned on her heels and walked away, yelling, "Keep it. I've lived without the stuff in that mausoleum for this long. I can live without it forever."

Jake looked down at the pathetic, sobbing man on the floor of the garage. Bruce's hands covered his eye as he yelled for Sophie. Pride filled Jake. She distanced herself from this ass of a man, and he had to admit that punch really turned him on. Amazed, he looked over and saw her hand on the handle of his truck door.

"You coming?" she asked with a smirk.

Jake jogged to the driver's side and jumped in. "Damn, girl! I was so hopin' to be the one to do that. But seeing your fist in his face was awesome." He turned and smiled at her, then for the hell of it, cupped her face and laid a quick kiss on her forehead.

"You're perverse, Jake. I like that." She returned his smile while he started the truck. "I feel bad that you came all the way out here with me for nothing."

"It wasn't for nothing." Jake pulled out of the drive and headed toward home. "You got to clock that son-of-a-bitch in the face."

She laughed a little, "Why, yes, I did."

"And feeling very proud of it."

"Why wouldn't I? My family taught me to put up with crap like that, and now that I've decided not to, it feels very liberating. My friend Kathy will be so proud. She hates him!"

"Your parents were for the two of you staying together?"

"My mother believes all men have their indiscretions. Although I don't think my father ever has. Me? I feel that if someone loves you enough, they'd never think about doing something so despicable."

"What does your mother think of that?"

"I'm crazy. And as soon as I stop acting like a child, I'll be lucky if Bruce forgives me and takes me back."

Jake swore. "I'm sorry, that's not cool at all. You'd think she'd want more for you."

"The women in my mother's family are known for being

doormats. I was one for too long. Bruce's affairs were such an embarrassment I thought I'd die. I could hear people whispering behind my back during practice and backstage at performances. Theatre is intimate and everyone knows your business. It was all very sad." She gave a wistful sigh, and Jake glanced at her. She looked hurt, and he wanted to take her in his arms to console her. His parents always let him know when they thought he was seeing someone who would be careless with his heart. They never steered him wrong, and he could trust them to always be there for him. The obvious strain Sophie had with her parents reminded Jake how truly lucky he was.

"Well, I would've never pictured you as a doormat. You certainly don't punch like one."

"Today's the first time I've punched someone since grade school, and I did it twice. Should I be proud of that?"

When she touched his shoulder Jake felt a rush of adrenaline, and his libido did a little jump. Deciding to change the subject to distract himself seemed to be the safest thing to do. "I wouldn't worry about it. How long did you dance for?"

"I was three when I started."

"Did you quit?"

"I have a dance hall where I practice every morning. But I don't dance professionally anymore."

"That's too bad. You didn't quit because of what happened with Bruce, did you? 'Cause that'd be pathetic."

"No." She folded her arms across her chest and looked out the window.

"I didn't mean to insult you. Just wondering why. I'm sure your parents have asked."

"They have."

When she said nothing else, Jake pulled into a restaurant. "I'm hungry, and it's been a good twenty hours since I've been able to keep anything down. You coming?" She looked at him with reservations, so he reassured her. "I promise I won't take advantage of you in there." He held up two fingers in the Boy Scout pledge.

"You were never a Boy Scout."

"Man, I was a Cub Scout, a Boy Scout, and an Eagle Scout, which is the highest honor," he told her while flicking a finger down her nose.

"And now you drink and pass out on the manager's couch. Were you partying for any particular reason?"

"My friend Mitch McCabe just had his first child. I told him I'd have a few for him."

Her smile bloomed beautifully across her face, and the spray of freckles on her nose caught the sunlight.

He asked, "Has anyone ever told you that you look like—?"

"Don't say it, Jake. I'm not big on being called cute."

"I wasn't going to say that. It's just…" He reached out and touched her soft cheek. Her doll-like eyes grew bigger than he thought possible. He wanted to kiss her. It must have been written on his face, because Sophie moved into his touch. Jake dropped his hand as the warning bells sounded. It had been so long, he'd be lucky if he remembered how to kiss. "Why don't we go in and get something to eat? All those physical altercations must have made you hungry."

Leaving her no choice, Jake jumped out of the truck before she could say anything. He didn't want to think of her as a woman or a prospective lover. Two years prior he had sworn to celibacy to help clear his mind and concentrate on what he needed to do next with his civilian life. Of course, he still hadn't figured out what "next" was.

Sophie looped her arm through his. "I quit because I didn't love it anymore. I hadn't in a long time." She stopped walking and pulled Jake so he'd look at her. "Just because you're talented at something doesn't mean it's what you have to do for the rest of your life. My heart wasn't in it long before Bruce's affairs. He and my parents pushed me to stay."

"I understand that."

"Is that how it was in the military?"

"How'd you know I was in the armed forces?"

She rolled her eyes. "Jake, I saw you naked. There's a tattoo on your upper right arm. Plus, there's Marine stuff all over your truck."

"Yeah, I guess it's a little hard to hide, eh? I left for personal reasons."

She saw a haunted look in his eyes before he began walking toward the entrance of the restaurant. Sophie sprinted to catch up. "Jake, I'm sorry."

"Stop saying that. I think you've apologized three times in this conversation and none of them were warranted. Geez, you never even said you were sorry for punching me."

"That's because you deserved it."

Her heart fluttered with excitement when he snickered at her. Jake had charisma and honesty, unlike most of the men Sophie knew. Her mind reeled back to when he touched her in the truck and the heat in his eyes when he stroked her cheek. She wondered what made him pull back so suddenly when it was obvious there was heat swilling between them. Was there a woman in his past, or something else?

"The only thing I deserve is a medal for not beating the living hell out of that ex of yours. Two, please," he told the hostess.

"This way." With a smile, the hostess showed them to a booth.

"Here are your menus and your waitress will be with you in a moment."

"Thank you." Sophie slid into her seat. "Bruce can get under your skin very easily," she told Jake.

"He's a pompous ass."

"I feel bad that I punched him." Sophie picked up her menu and opened it. "You know, there was a time when walking into a place like this wouldn't have happened. As a dancer you have to keep a strict diet."

"I can't imagine."

"No, you can't. And, seeing that I'm more filled out than most dancers, I really had to keep control." She saw his eyes wander over her.

"I like your curves."

Sophie smiled and took a chance at being flirtatious. "I like yours, too, Mr. Sanders." At the faint color in his cheeks Sophie felt a power she hadn't known a woman could possess. Testing, Sophie leaned over to let her breasts rest on the table. Her shirt swooped low at the collar and she knew she was giving Jake a nice view. "Tell me why you don't have a woman."

"I do. Her name is Trixie." She saw the telltale signs of a nervous man when he swallowed hard.

"Ready to order?" their bubbly waitress with a big-toothed smile asked.

"Yes, I'll have the chicken cobb salad and water," Sophie said.

Jake smirked, "Livin' dangerous with that one, Sophie. How about we order a meat lover's pizza?"

Sophie placed her hand on her stomach. "Aggg, no thanks. I'd have to pick up ginger ale and antacids on the way home to settle my stomach. I'll stick with the salad."

"A large steak—medium to well—with mashed potatoes,

no salad, and a pitcher of Coke," Jake told the waitress with a wink.

"You do know that I made up Trixie, right?" Sophie asked Jake when the waitress left.

His eyes lit up and his laugh was joyful. "Really?"

"Really. I actually came up with that. Not the guy you were trying to beat earlier."

"Are you flirting with me, Sophie?"

"Maybe. Why, is that wrong?"

Jake sat back and studied her. "I'm off the market." His phone began to vibrate on the table and he picked it up. "Yup...No, everything is fine...Okay, talk to ya later." Hanging up, he smiled at Sophie. "Dave wanted to make sure we were good."

Sophie's ever-inquisitive brain rewound to Jake telling Bruce the only woman he'd been around in a while was Trixie. "Really, off the market? Because at the bar the men were all talking about how you haven't been laid in years." She snorted when Jake gave her a bland stare. "There has to be a story here. Tell me."

Jake played with the straw in his soda. "You don't miss anything, do you? Maybe some other time I'll spill my guts. Right now I don't want to ruin our good moment."

"Okay. Then tell me how you and your brother opened the Hungry Lion." From his sad look, Sophie realized this man's scars were deeper than the ones on his perfectly chiseled body—a body she desperately wanted to get her hands on.

"I was on leave from the war when my brother had been talkin' about opening a restaurant. So, I thought, why not? I knew when I got home for good I'd need something to do."

"What exactly do you do? Besides screw up the books?" Jake reached across the table and flicked her nose; she laughed and swatted his hand.

"I told you they were like that when I got them. I'm actually very good with my money. I just don't have the head for business. How did you get involved in this type of thing?"

"I took business classes despite my parents' and Bruce's disapproval. I'm glad it's paying off now that I quit dancing."

"But you worked someplace else before us? Thank you," he said to the waitress as she placed the food in front of him.

Sophie's body heated as she watched Jake cut and then fork steak into his mouth. What would those full masculine lips feel like on her breasts?

"Ummm...Yeah...The job really sucked, though. My boss was a total wretch. At first I didn't want to leave because I knew my parents would say, 'See? You need to be a dancer.' But that's not what I want. I like the accounting, advertising, and everything else that goes with it. Sounds silly, doesn't it?"

"Nope."

Sophie studied him for a few seconds. He was an intimidating man, yet she never felt threatened by him. When she looked deeper into his eyes, she realized he'd moved the conversation off of him and on to her.

"So, Jake."

"Yes."

"What is it you do for the business?"

He laughed heartily and wagged a finger at her. "You got me."

"Yes, I did. You changed the subject very smoothly. Was that helpful in the Marines?"

"It came in handy. I don't do anything for the business. For the last few years I've needed to take care of a few things. When Dave asked me to take over on the books, I suggested hiring someone."

"You needed to take care of a few things." Sophie took a large bite of her salad. She contemplated the man in front of her while taking her time chewing. "The last time I had to 'take care of something,' it was code for 'myself.' Did you find what you were looking for?"

"Maybe. You?"

She leaned forward, looked straight into his eyes, and said, "Yup."

Chapter 4

So what do you think of her?" Dave asked with a raised eyebrow.

Jake eyed his brother as he pumped iron. "What's there to think?"

"What happened when you guys went out to eat?"

"Nothing, Dave." Jake's voice strained as he lifted one more time, and Dave helped him place the barbell in its rack. "We had a great conversation and that's it."

"A great conversation? Sounds kinda boring."

Jake turned to his brother with a huff. "She asked if I'm involved with anyone," he said while swiping sweat from his brow

"Really? What did you say?"

"What the hell do you think I said?" Jake scowled at the floor. "I told her I am."

"Jake, you're my brother, and that's why I think I can be honest with you. You're screwin' up your life for nothing."

"It's not for nothing. And it's my choice."

"You're really going to let that bitch ruin your life?"

"That's not fair, Dave. It's not just because of her, there's other things, too." Jake stretched his arms across his broad chest.

"Damn, Jake. All you do is work out, eat, read, work out, eat, read. When's the last time you've had some fun?"

"A few days ago when I woke up naked in the manager's office. I still don't know how I got that way." Jake gave Dave a mischievous grin.

"Too bad Trixie didn't take advantage of you."

"Yeah, sometimes I miss that."

"Well, at least I know the parts still work if you're missing it."

"Thanks, Dave." Jake slugged his water and thought of the temperamental dancer with the big eyes. He hadn't yearned for the company of a woman in so long that the sensation seemed foreign. Heck, what man wouldn't want to be around her? She was beautiful, had a wicked sense of humor. Her slow smiles always brought butterflies swarming in his stomach, and he sometimes found himself stumbling over his own tongue when talking to her. If he was looking for a good time—which, he assured himself, he wasn't—he would definitely be sniffin' around Sophie. She had looks, personality, all the right assets and…his body stirred and his loins began to throb. *Shit.* He really needed to think of old women, hairy men, and gross, rotten food. Otherwise, he was going to give everybody in the gym a show of his manhood.

"So Jake, now that there's a manager in the office taking over your job, are you going to stop comin' around?"

Jake shrugged. "Naw, I think I might stand behind the bar a few hours every night. Give myself something to do."

"Or the opportunity to look at someone?"

"Dave, I'm really not interested."

"Whatever you say." Dave shrugged. "I gotta go. See ya later?"

"Yeah, sure."

Jake turned back to the workout machines behind him. Maybe

he did spend too much time there. What else did he have to do? After everything was settled, Jake found himself without the woman he loved, short a kidney, and with no place to belong. For a while he thought about traveling, but the prospect of doing it alone seemed depressing. What kind of good time can a solo person have when haunted memories follow him wherever he goes?

He pushed through the locker room doors and went for the showers. The strong smell of powder and ammonia triggered Jake's mind instantly to the notion of sterilization, hospitals, and wounds. He fought with the storm cloud trying to blanket his consciousness. He knew what came next, and he desperately fought to stay in reality.

The shower spray felt good on his skin. Purifying his soul as his memories manifested themselves into a hallucination. Jake was back in the hole. He could feel the weight of his armor and weapons as he crouched down to stay hidden from his squad's objective.

Without warning a flash of bright light blinded him while a piercing sound left him deaf for what seemed like an eternity. Jake covered his ears and went down to his knees as water sprayed over him, much like the dirt that rained down in his delusion. Gasping for air, Jake forced his mind to see reality instead of the moment that changed him forever. He looked down at his hands; water ran through his fingers much like the blood had when he rolled one of his comrades over to check for life. It was then he knew he was in trouble. All his men were wounded or dead.

What the hell happened? Why did I live? He asked the questions over and over again, but the answers always eluded him. The plan had been to get in as quietly as possible then out the same way. But wasn't that always the plan? Except, this time the adversary had been waiting for them, as if they'd known.

Jake pondered many nights wondering if there'd been a mole. Each time the answer came back no. It was only a line of attack gone wrong, plain and simple. But Jake never made a plan that didn't work out perfectly. He was the best at what he did, and he couldn't accept that this time he hadn't been right about the strategy. He was missing the whole story, and his subconscious wouldn't let him see what his mind wanted to show him.

Jake came back to reality wedged in the corner of the shower stall. His body shook violently while he tried, once again, to clear the illusion before him. This time it worked, and he found himself exhausted. Turning off the water, Jake rested his head against the cool ceramic tile. He evened his breathing and did a mental check of himself—every limb still attached and no wounds visible. Standing with shoulders rolled back and his head high, Jake walked into the quiet locker room and dressed. His body dragged while his mind tried to clear. Jake hadn't experienced a flashback in a long time, and with each one he bounced back a little bit better and remembered a little more about the night his life changed. "Pieces to a puzzle," his therapist told him. "When your mind is ready, they will all fit together and you will remember."

Jake scrubbed his hands over his face and told himself, "Gut up, Gunny. Gut up. You're alive."

* * *

Sophie knocked on the door enthusiastically. She didn't know how he would hear her with all the noise coming from the small house. She recognized the tune and sang along in her mind as she waited for an answer.

The plan had been a simple one: go to Dave's and find out the password to the company computer, go home and talk to Kathy for a while, then soak in a deep bath of bubbles with Mozart playing softly in the background. Instead, Sophie discovered, after an hour of trying to contact Dave, that Jake had changed the password when he took the finances over, and Dave had it "written down somewhere"—but it would be easier if she just asked Jake.

"HA." She laughed at the lunacy of it all because now it was Jake who wouldn't answer his phone or door. "How the heck did they run this business without me?" she asked herself.

At first Sophie hesitated, then with more effort than needed, she pushed his door open and called to him. Realizing she couldn't be heard over the music, Sophie searched out the source of the riot. In his living room she found a huge fifty-two-inch DSL television and a state-of-the-art music system. Next to it were stacks of CDs, which, after closer inspection, looked all to be in alphabetical order. *Little OCD, Jake?* With a tentative hand, she found the Off switch to the music system and felt the vibrations in her body cease immediately, but the ringing in her ears continued.

"It's like being at a damn concert," she murmured to herself.

"That's the way I like it. What the hell are you doing in my house?"

At his deep voice, Sophie screamed and jumped around with a hand to her chest. "You could have let me know you were there!"

"I just did," Jake said.

His smile infuriated her, but she couldn't say if the blush she felt on her cheeks came from fury or from the fact Jake stood before her half-naked. Jean shorts rode low on his hips, his top button was undone, and his chest was bare. She eyed the long scar across his torso and wondered how it could make him look sexier.

"You do realize its fifty degrees outside, right?"

"Yeah, I'm warm-blooded. Why are you here?"

She watched as he approached her. His effortless saunter gave her the impression of a panther in the moonlight. His eyes were dark and intense, as the shadows of the ending day gave his face a dangerous appeal. What had she gotten herself into? Did she really think she could handle this man? He stopped within inches of her. The powerful animal magnetism between them gave way to a low purr escaping Sophie's throat.

"I've never felt this intense of an attraction toward someone before. I'm not quite sure what to do with it," he told her.

She went with her desire and brought a hand up to his chest. Sophie watched in fascination as his muscles jumped at her touch. "You have the most incredible body."

"Please." He took a sharp breath and twined his fingers in her hair. "Sophie, please stop."

"But you're pulling me to you." She gazed up into eyes that looked as confused as she felt. "I don't understand, Jake."

"I'm only playing in good fun, Sophie. I'm—"

"—not involved with anyone." She stepped forward so their bodies brushed. "We work at the same place, remember?" Feeling daring, Sophie stretched up to her toes and nibbled on his chin.

"I don't think this is a smart idea." He shifted his face to nuzzle her neck. "I really don't want to start any kind of—"

"Don't tell me you've never done something that wasn't part of a plan," she whispered.

"I...yes, no...Damn, I can't think."

"Where's your brain, Sergeant?" He smelled amazingly male, and the touch of his lips on her neck and ears combined the sensations together to create a firestorm of need. She hadn't stopped thinking about him or their meal at the restaurant. The connection developing between them seemed to grow stronger, even in their absence from each another.

"Gunnery Sergeant, and it went south along with all my blood."

Daring herself to be bolder, Sophie told him what she felt. "You know, Jake, I didn't come here with this intention. Yet I always seem to find you without clothes on, and it's making me do things I would never ever think of doing with someone I barely know. This is crazy. I can't stop thinking about you."

With his hands on her shoulders, Jake stood her at arm's length and stared deep into her eyes. "I'm going to go put a shirt on."

Sophie took a deep breath. "Okay, maybe you're right. Space, breathing room, umm—" She smiled to herself when he turned and appeared to sprint away. That was her first instinct, too, but what was the use in running when they would only find themselves pulled together again? As her thoughts processed, she wandered into the kitchen, where a large pot on the stove held simmering sauce. Next to it, his spice cabinet door was left open, showing all the jars were displayed smallest to tallest, faced forward and in alphabetical order.

"You're very organized, Jake."

"I like knowing where things are. There's nothing wrong with that."

Sophie looked at the spice jars. "I suppose not. Could you come and organize my kitchen? It's a mess."

"Sure, why not. I was just about to make some pasta. You want some?"

Jake reached up and closed the cabinet with a slam while he pulled his other hand through his hair. He looked a little uncomfortable with her standing in his kitchen, so Sophie stepped back to give him more room and mustered up the courage to ask, "Are you asking me to dinner, Jake?"

"After you tried to molest me in my own living room I should kick you out on that firm ass of yours, but I won't."

"I wasn't the only one doing the molesting, big boy." Playing, Sophie went for a grab at the front of his shirt and Jake maneuvered away from her.

"Hands to yourself, little lady."

"Okay, but you started it." She turned back to the stove and picked up the spoon next to the pot.

"Here, let me."

Sophie connected her eyes with his when he brought the spoon of sauce to her lips. She blew gently then tasted. "Mmm. Jake, this is delicious." When she licked her lips, Jake rolled his eyes to the ceiling.

"Why am I in this situation?" He gently wiped stray sauce from the side of her mouth. "I should be concentrating on so many other things," he told her after licking the sauce off his thumb.

"Maybe you're just attracted to dancing accountants," she laughed.

"Never was before," he said with a smirk. "It could be interesting." With haste, he grabbed a pot from the hanging rack above the stove and filled it with water. "So, have you heard from your friend?"

"Friend?"

"The one with the fresh black eye."

"Ohhh. Yeah, he called my parents and they called me. My mother is disappointed I showed my anger. Apparently, it wasn't very ladylike of me to lose my temper."

"I thought it was one of the sexiest things I've ever seen." He salted the boiling water then added some oil.

"I'll let her know that next time I talk to her. My father was more concerned with 'the bar' I'm presently working at."

Jake grinned at her, "It's not really a bar."

"I know. But they don't understand that."

Jake leaned against the counter and watched her. "What are you doing here?"

"Having supper."

"Sophie..."

"I needed the password for the computer. Dave didn't know it." She smiled and batted her eyes lashes at him.

* * *

Jake turned to stir the pasta while shaking his head. "You have the most beautiful smile."

"Really? Thank you." Sophie walked to the kitchen hutch and started looking at the photos set next to the dishes on the shelves. "But it doesn't seem to have an effect on you."

"What makes you say that? Because I didn't throw you on the couch and make love to you?" He wanted to. Lord knows how much he wanted to. But after so many years of celibacy, Jake found himself as nervous as a teenage boy in the backseat of a car for the first time.

"Well, yeah."

He felt her move toward him, so he turned and pointed at her with a grin on his lips. "You said you wouldn't touch me."

"I'm not going to," she told him, tongue in cheek.

Her playful demeanor made his nerves dance, awakening his libido. When she took the wooden spoon from him and smacked the side of his butt cheek he yelled, "Hey! What are you doing?"

"Spanking you."

The glint in her eyes made Jake rethink the living room couch, but the kitchen counters were closer. Instead, he grabbed the spoon back and smacked her ass good. "How'd that feel?"

She leaned forward so their lips were a whisper apart. "Wonderful."

"You're driving me nuts, Sophie. Listen...I'm just going to be right up front with you. I haven't been with a woman in two years."

One of her eyebrows lifted. "Is there someone you wanted to be with?"

"No."

Her bottom lip puffed out, just a tiny bit. "I'm screwing that up, aren't I?"

He studied her. She wasn't questioning his confession, but she didn't ask why, either. He found that fact very interesting. "Yes, you are messing it up."

"Well, I guess it's a good thing I promised not to touch you anymore." She smiled at him. "I think you need to drain that spaghetti, Jake."

Looking down, he saw the pasta was almost overdone. "Right. Umm, it was a personal decision."

"Did it have to do with the things you needed 'to take care of'?" She opened cabinet doors until she found dishware for them to eat off of.

"Yeah." He wasn't sure how ready he was to talk about something so private, but without her pushing it seemed he could go at his own pace. "You want mozzarella on this?"

"Yes, please."

He spooned two bowls of pasta and sauce with fresh grated cheese and brought them to the table. When they were settled, Jake looked into her eyes to search her soul. He saw she had been waiting for him to talk. "When I got back from the war I was wounded, a little messed up in the head, and my girlfriend left me for her boss. They'd made plans to marry while I was deployed. I mean *real* plans. The dress, church, reception, honeymoon, you name it, it was all in order. All I had to do was get home so she could tell me. But seeing that I came home early with a few bullets, she offered to postpone the wedding."

Surprise and detest crossed Sophie's features. "Wow. That was very sweet of the hussy."

Despite himself, Jake laughed. "Yeah, I guess you're right there. Anyway, she was married for about a year when she realized that she really did love me."

"This just keeps getting better. Let me guess." Sophie batted her lashes and made a sad puppy dog face, then sniffled, "Jake, I'm sooo sorry. I was lonely and he comforted me when you weren't here. But, I was thinking of you every time... what's his name?"

"Asshole."

"Every time Asshole and I were together. Can you forgive me and take me back?"

"No!" Jake said, smirking. Then he did something he never thought possible. He reached across the table and cupped Sophie's chin in one of his hands as he stretched over to her, seconds before their lips touched. The kiss was sweet and over before it even began, but it left Jake muddled. Sophie must have been muddled, too, because her eyes looked mildly shocked.

"I didn't touch you," she told him.

"No, you didn't. Thank you for understanding."

"Kiss me one more time and I won't tease you for the rest of the meal."

"How about just because I want to?"

She shrugged, and Jake asked himself how her mere presence could cause him to feel and try things that he had wanted to do for years. He brought his lips back to hers, but this time he moved his hand from her chin to the back of her head. He kissed her deeper and longer, allowing his body to respond how it wanted. No, he hadn't forgotten how to do this, and it felt wonderful having his lips on hers. Their tongues danced, and he felt her hand on his cheek.

"You're touching me," he said against her mouth.

"I can't help it," she whispered. "You're lucky I'm not pulling you over this table and ripping off your clothes."

Jake rested his forehead on hers. "If you're a good girl, maybe someday I'll let you."

Chapter 5

Hey, Gunny. How do you like working for your big brother?" Louie teased.

"Who said I'm working for him?" Jake's eyes wandered to the office down the hall. As he wiped down the beer counter he wondered if she would ever come out. Sophie had been hiding in there all week "organizing." He didn't realize there was so much to do. In his mind, she needed only to look at the books, make some changes to how they spent their money, and then rearrange a few things. Nothing to it. Then again, that could have been why they hired her, because Dave and him were doing just that, and it wasn't working.

"So, who are you working for if it isn't your brother?"

Jake's attention went back to his customer, who practically lived at the Hungry Lion. "I work only for myself, and don't let anyone tell you otherwise."

"Actually, he works for me, now."

Jake turned to the lyrical sound of Sophie's voice. She looked really pretty today in her baggy jeans and low-cut orange shirt. Without thinking, he began to admire her chest and she snapped her fingers at him.

"My face is up here, Jake," she said with a snicker.

He felt the heat in his cheeks. "Sorry. You can be very distracting."

"Where's Dave?"

"Why?" He wanted her to stay out in the open longer. It would give him the opportunity to smell her sweet scent and look at her a little more.

"I need to talk to him about an advertising thing."

"Why can't you talk to me?" She rolled her eyes at Jake, causing him to tighten his grip on a glass. If he squeezed any harder, he was certain it would break.

"You're a silent partner, and Dave asked that I talk with him about all promotion decisions."

She licked her lips, an involuntary movement, causing a sexual tension to coil through Jake's body. One half of him wanted to push her away, while the other became desperate to throw her atop the bar and have his way with her.

"I can make decisions," he told her.

"Okay, how about a Halloween party with giveaways? It would bring traffic in, and I've been thinking about a new menu for the kitchen. Something a little more festive like Ghouls Stew and Eyeball Salad?"

"Well, I don't know what Ghouls Stew is, but yeah, I think the party sounds cool." He winked at her then grabbed another glass to dry. He knew he shouldn't be thinking about her so much. The night they kissed at his house was the first time in years he'd felt a real passionate pull toward a woman. He'd told himself that sooner or later he would develop an attraction to someone. However, he never imagined it would be like this, and with someone like Sophie. All the women he previously dated didn't have the strength, drive, or compassion she did. They also didn't propel him to protect them emotionally as well as physically, like Sophie did. Why else would he have gone along for the ride to her summer home?

It was all kind of scary, and the uneasiness he felt stood rooted in the fact that he let down everyone he ever cared about. First, he sent his military team straight into an ambush and to their deaths. Second, he couldn't hold on to his fiancée because he hadn't had the ability to give her the emotional support she needed, and that had pushed her into the arms of another man.

Then there was his family. Jake had always been the good son. His parents were so proud of him when he joined the Marines and worked his way up the ranks. When he came back broken they offered to sell their retirement home in Florida and move back, but Jake insisted they didn't. They had always been understanding and loving, and letting them give up what they had worked so hard for would have been just another way he let them down.

Jake wasn't a man they could rely on anymore. He wasn't the guy who could make everything better. The baggage he carried was too heavy and too painful for him to help someone else with theirs, and that was why he couldn't even think about being intimate with Sophie.

Jake looked down at the small delicate hand that wrapped only partway around his bicep. Her baby blue eyes and naked pink lips beckoned him to kiss her again.

"What?" he asked, a little shaken by everything he felt.

"You okay?"

The concern in her eyes let an honest smile form on his lips. "Now, how could I not be with a beautiful lady by my side?" For this comment, Jake received whoops and howlers from his regulars.

"True." She sauntered off and Jake gave a warning look to the man in front of him who leered at her from his stool.

"Louie, I wouldn't think about it," he told him.

"I was just looking."

"Yeah, well, I don't want you doing that, either."

"Doing what?" Dave came around the corner of the bar and gave Jake a nod.

"I think our Jake has a thing for the new chick. It's kinda cute, being his first crush and all." Louie held up his hands in defeat when Jake sneered at him.

"I won't hurt you this time," Jake told the man. "But, if any more crap comes out of your mouth, I'll be forced to wipe the floor with you . . . again."

"Jake, be nice to our customers or I'll have your new girlfriend fire you."

"All of you suck!" Jake threw down the dry cloth and walked toward the backroom. He could hear the men taunting him as he went. She wasn't his girlfriend—not even close. All Sophie could be was a woman of interest. So what if she was feisty and built like a brick shithouse? So what if she made him think of garter belts and lace panties worn with stilettos? She was a woman, that was all.

He walked into her office where she was found bent over, her sweet ass in the air, picking something up. The thought of his hands on her bottom and his tongue tasting between those long, toned legs made Jake swear aloud and Sophie turn with a puzzled look.

"What's up?" she asked, and went back to digging through the box in front of her.

"You're not my girlfriend," he said, more forcefully than needed.

"Oh, thank God you told me. I was just thinking about picking out dinnerware." She straightened and worked some kinks out of her back.

"I don't want any type of relationship. I've been solo for years and I don't need the complication in my life."

One of her eyebrows came up in a question. Jake couldn't deny the sexiness of the movement or his physical reaction to it. Emotions swamped him in a chaotic jumble. Everything about her beaconed a warning, as a lighthouse would to caution ships headed for the rocky shores. Lord help him. How would he survive?

"Okay. I hadn't realized we were headed that way. If it happens again, please let me know." She smiled and sauntered over to him. "Jake. I'm not going to molest you. Unless that's what you want."

"I don't want you to do anything." He took in a ragged breath as his hands stroked up her sides to rest around his neck.

"Then I'll let you do it all," she said, while flipping her hair behind her back.

"You're not playing fair." He nuzzled her neck and tugged on her earlobe with his teeth. "Coming in smelling sweet and looking beautiful. You're seducing me, Sophie." One of his hands firmly cupped her butt and brought her tight against his groin.

"Just remember, I'm not touching you... but I really want to." Her voice turned thick with passion. He heard it and realized his voice must sound the same.

Needing more, but not completely sure he would be able to handle her, Jake quietly demanded, "Touch me." The instant his words were out Sophie's hand shot between them and began to massage him through his jeans. Emotions filled his body and mind. Sensations, which long lay dormant, awakened with

Sophie's very existence in his world. How could he explain to her that the war inside of him retreated every time she was near? That each day he learned to feel again, to *live*? Fervor raced through him while the world spun around. Jake gasped for air as his control started to slip.

Sophie kissed his neck and whispered in his ear, "I've never been so forward with a man before. I can't seem to contain myself around you."

"I don't seem to have control, either." His body trembled. Restraint…he needed to find it before he exploded from the friction her hand was creating. "Wait, Sophie, I—" She stopped without question, and looking as startled as he felt, took a step away from him. "I'm sorry, Sophie. It must seem like I'm teasing you." Shame filled him, and he bit his lower lip to keep the vulgar words he wanted to call himself quiet.

"Jake." She placed a gentle hand to his cheek. "You've been through a hell of a lot. Don't worry, I'll be here when you're ready."

"I really want to say the hell with all of it and—"

"Hey, what's going on in here?" Dave stood there, looking from Jake to Sophie.

"I was just letting Sophie know that I was leaving for the night."

"Really?"

"What's the matter, Dave?" Sophie went back to her box, but this time she squatted down. "Feeling like you're missing out on something?" She turned and winked at him.

"Yeah. He walks in here and doesn't come out for ten minutes. I have to wonder if he's passed out on your couch." Dave gave his brother a good-natured slap on the back.

"Ha ha. Very funny. Okay, I'm out for the day."

Jake left without looking at either of them, or the customers with their questioning eyes. He had made a fool of himself
and was positive Sophie was the reason for it. What happened
to the smooth-talking guy who had women falling all over him?
Or, the man who could, and did, take any woman he wanted
to bed?

He got fucked. That was what happened. The woman he was
going to marry ran away with someone else. The sting might still
be there, but somehow it wasn't as sharp as it once was. Maybe
time *did* heal all things. Maybe he *would* get laid again. Jake
laughed at himself. Only a desperate man would be compar-
ing love wounds to having sex. Yet he found himself wanting
more than that quick physical release. No, he didn't want only a
body to plunder. He craved laughing, quiet smiles, private jokes
shared between two people who've been intimate. He thought
about what it would be like to have Sophie in bed. Those glori-
ous breasts, muscular body, and fiery personality would be lethal.
But at least he'd die a happy man.

* * *

Sophie giggled when Jake was out of earshot, high on her new-
found sexual power and the fact she had never affected a man
like this before. She found it quite fun that he had the same
influence on her as she did over him. Being around Jake sent her
into a physical and mental need. She wanted to joke with him
and talk about everything and nothing at the same time. It was
an exciting comfort she'd never experienced with a man before.
"That man is a mess, Dave."

"Sophie."

When she looked at Dave, she knew what he would say next.

"I'm not playing with him. Actually, I'm not quite sure what's going on."

"It's been a long time since my baby brother was involved with anyone. I keep a close eye on him."

"I know, Dave. Jake is an amazing man. He told me about his ex and that he hasn't been with a woman in a long time. It seems like he's interested, but he keeps giving me mixed signals. First he kisses me, then tells me he doesn't want a relationship, but finishes the conversation with…well…you get the point. I don't really know where I stand with him, but I'm willing to give him the time to figure out what he wants." She sat behind her desk.

"Sophie, there're some things you need to know."

"Dave, I don't think Jake will appreciate us gossiping about him."

"I'm only watching out for the both of you. Sophie, look at me."

She studied Dave's stark expression, no longer feeling humorous. "What is it, Dave?"

"Jake came back a mess."

"I know that."

"No, you don't. You've heard about the girl and the bullets, plus the fire at his apartment. You didn't hear about the downward spiral he had eight months after being home. It was so gradual that at first no one noticed. Then he found out one of our childhood friends died, and he hit bottom hard. Jake and Chuck were real close growing up. Heck, they even joined the military together. After a few years they lost track of each other but met up again while stationed in Afghanistan." Dave went silent for a moment inner pain displayed prominently on his face. "Chuck was still active when Jake came home. I thought if I contacted him it would cheer Jake up. He took his girlfriend marrying another man really hard."

"I think I would, too."

Dave sat down on the couch. His hands dangled between his legs while he gave his shoulders a helpless shrug. "Chuck had killed himself only days before, and his family hadn't contacted Jake yet."

Sophie's breath clogged her lungs. Never would she be able to imagine the anguish Jake lived through the past few years. It wasn't fair. A man who fought for his country, put his life on the line to protect the rights of others, and this is how he's repaid? The very idea of it left Sophie dumbfounded. "Why? How?"

"Chuck dressed in full military uniform, shined his shoes, oiled his gun, and blew his head off. A seemingly normal man who looked as if he had it all together did the unthinkable. He'd been suffering from PTSD. It's what Jake has now."

"Oh, God." A feeling of helplessness for Jake and Chuck overwhelmed her. What could she do to help Jake? Did she really want to be involved with someone who had those types of problems? She didn't even know where to start or what to do.

Dave's face went grim. "Post-traumatic stress disorder is a serious thing."

She tried waving his concern away in hopes that it wasn't as bad as he was making it out to be. "Dave, I've been around Jake. He's working, talking, living on his own—"

Dave shook his head. "You don't get it. That's how it is, until something triggers it. For Jake it was the death of his friend and comrades. If you want to be with him and be a part of his life, you need to understand that the man went to hell and came back not whole. He doesn't feel like we do. He can't watch horror movies. Loud bangs or backfires from cars cause him to drop to the ground. When he came home and all the bullshit was sorted through, he lived hour to hour, because there was no other way for him. Nightmares, loss of time, mood swings. I've seen him have a flashback just from smelling something. Sophie, tread carefully. You can't imagine the things he's been through."

"No, I can't. Has he talked to you about it?" She felt a little sick and placed a hand on her stomach in hopes of calming it down.

"No, he says it's too much for me to hear about and understand. Truthfully, I don't think I want to know what Jake saw. I'm not a strong enough person for that." Clearly agitated, he stood and paced the room. "Most people aren't. All I know is he came home with pictures of dead bodies in his head and time missing. I woke him up out of a nightmare once and thought he was gonna kill me. Not because I woke him, but because he was still there battling the war." Dave went quiet. His concern so evident it made Sophie's heart ache. "Jake always wanted to be a Marine. He was born for it. It was something he had to do. It takes a special person to be married to the military, and someone even more exceptional to have a relationship with that person. Sophie, you need to think about this."

She remained silent for a moment. Alone in her thoughts about a man she, for some reason, couldn't stop thinking about or wanting to be near. The connection they had only seemed to be getting stronger, and now Dave was really giving her something to think about if she planned on pursuing him. "I'm sorry, Dave. I had no idea."

"I know. That's why I wanted to tell you. If there's anything you need to ask, don't hesitate. Jake isn't open with many people." Dave smiled, "He seems to have taken to you, though."

"I've taken to him, and I promise to do everything I can not to hurt him." Sophie picked at a loose thread on her shirt. "You're a really good brother for looking out for Jake. I wish I had someone to do that for me."

"No one watched out for you, Sophie?"

"Only a few good friends. I was an only child, unfortunately." She picked up a stack of papers on her desk and tapped them even. She really needed to process everything Dave had told her. The problem was she'd already started to care for Jake. But did she see herself loving him? She wanted him in the worst way, yet somehow she knew sex wouldn't be enough. For either of them. "Okay, fun time's over. I have some advertising ideas I want to go over with you. I spoke to Jake about it earlier, but the only thing I got was him staring at my breasts."

Dave smirked, "Always was a breast man."

She pressed her lips together in an attempt to stifle her laughter. "Okay, how about a Halloween party? I think we can put it together in three weeks." The chair squeaked as Sophie turned to the computer.

"Let's do it."

"Oh, and I need a new office chair."

"I think we can budget that."

When the soft knock on the door sounded, both yelled, "Come in!" A dark-haired woman stuck her head inside.

"Hi," she said with a soft-as-a-feather voice. Sophie noticed the instant blush when her friend looked at Dave.

"Kathy, come in. This is Dave. Dave, my friend Kathy."

Dave stood mesmerized by the woman who walked in the door.

"Dave? You okay?"

"What? Oh…yeah. Hi." He extended a hand to Kathy, who fidgeted before she shook it.

"I'm not interrupting anything, am I?"

"Don't be silly. Dave and I were talking about holding a Halloween party here. What do you think?"

"Umm. Well, with the right advertising and door prizes, you could really bring in a killing." Kathy's eyes went from Sophie's to Dave's then to the floor.

"Kathy's an accountant," Sophie said to Dave.

"Was," Kathy added weakly. "They laid me off last year."

Dave took a step forward and cocked his head. "That sucks. The economy has really affected too many people. Are you lookin'?"

"Yes."

"No luck?"

"No." Kathy snuck a peek at Dave from under her lashes. "Hopefully soon though," she said, smiling.

Sophie saw Dave let out a long breath he must have been holding. Feeling the need to help the two of them out she asked, "Well, Dave, would you mind if Kathy and I have a break together?"

"No, not at all," he said while watching Kathy. "Why don't you order some food and sit out in a booth?"

Kathy accepted the invitation with a hesitant smile. "Thank you."

Sophie observed Dave as he led Kathy out with one hand placed at the small of her back. Dave leaned down close and whispered something in Kathy's ear, and she responded with a low laugh. Having never seen Dave flirt with a woman, Sophie admired how smooth he seemed to be, and how much Kathy enjoyed the attention. It wasn't often you got to see two people so taken with each other right from the moment they met. She wondered if Kathy should come around more often. There was nothing wrong with doing a little matchmaking.

Sophie slid into the booth across from her friend. Kathy's face was beet red, her eyes focused on the table. "He asked me if I'm seeing anyone," she told Sophie in a whisper.

"Really? What'd you say?"

"I have a date this weekend." Disappointment showed in Kathy's eyes as she looked up.

"You could always cancel."

"Oh, no! This is our second one, and I asked for it." Kathy tugged on her ear. "I said if it doesn't work out, I'll let him know. Do you think that was too forward?"

Sophie laughed despite the seriousness in Kathy's voice. "No. I think you might finally be coming out of your little cocoon, is all. Dave's a great guy."

"Then why don't *you* date him?"

"Because his brother is more my type." At Sophie's declaration, Kathy gave her a disgusted look. "Okay. My new type," she clarified.

"Can't wait to meet him. Is he here?"

"Ladies, here's your appetizers." Dave set down the plates and winked at Kathy. "If there's anything else you want, let me know."

"Don't worry, Dave," Sophie cooed. "I won't tell Kathy about your many exploits with loose women."

Dave looked at her with narrowed eyes. "Now why would you want to make things up about me? Loose women," he scoffed. "That's more Jake's territory."

Kathy smiled mischievously. "So, I hear Sophie is scoping on your brother. We all know what a vixen she's turned into."

Dave looked at Kathy with astonishment as Sophie laughed. "Don't look so shocked, Dave. This girl can insult you and you'll walk away smiling because you didn't realize it. She's not as quiet and innocent as she leads you to believe."

"Really?" was his only reply. He slipped into the booth next to Kathy.

"Apparently, I'm a very bad influence on Sophie. At least, according to her parents."

"Really?" Dave picked up Kathy's hand and kissed it. "I'd like to know what kind of persuasion you'd have on me."

"She's a real live witch, Dave. Be careful what you wish for," Sophie teased.

"Yes, Dave." In an uncharacteristic and daring move, Kathy brought her face close to his. "I can make you fall in love with one small chant."

"I think you already did."

Chapter 6

"If I ignore her she'll go away," Jake told his reflection in the mirror as he dressed for the Halloween party. He had to admit it was a good idea. They had sold hundreds of tickets, and the door prizes were phenomenal.

Jake adjusted his pirate shirt. He looked good, even if he was a little biased thinking it about himself. He wondered what Sophie would be going as, then dismissed the thought. He probably wouldn't see her the entire night. Not with all the people and events going on. Plus, working behind the bar wouldn't give him much time to stare at her like he had become accustomed to doing. He liked the way she would turn and smile at him with a wink. It always seemed like she knew something he didn't. Like there was a secret he needed to figure out, because she wasn't going to tell him.

Just as he was about to grab his car keys a knock sounded at the door. "Coming!" He opened it to an extremely sexy Tinker Bell. Sophie's hair was now blond, and the tiny green outfit accented not only her eyes but every curve of her body.

"Oh, God," Jake yipped, and closed the door in her face. With his back leaning up against it, he heard the knocking again.

"Jake! This isn't funny! Your brother disappeared again, and I can't find my keys to open up for the band. I know you're not supposed to be there for another half hour, but—"

He cut her off by opening the door. "Sorry," he laughed, "I was just on my way there. Thought I'd show up early. Wow, you look great." His eyes roamed her from head to toe and back again.

"Thanks, you look delicious, too. Can I have the key?" She placed a hand on her cocked hip and batted her eyes at him.

"Shit." Jake swung her into the house and pressed her back against the now-closed front door. His mouth feasted her welcoming lips. The powerful need inside him drove Jake beyond the rational and into the realm of his deepest fantasies. The potent flavors she emanated commanded him to taste her face and neck, and he always came back to those luscious lips. His body was on fire, and she stoked it to a blaze. "How do you do it? How do you make me feel this way? Don't stop, please." His hands squeezed her bottom while his lips moved to her breast.

"Jake, we have to go," Sophie panted.

"I know. But, you have no idea what you do to me," he said against her chest while grinding his hips into hers. "Just one more kiss."

The rush she gave him overpowered his every thought. Without her he felt nothing—with her, he felt everything. He didn't know whether to run away or fall to his knees and thank Sophie for bringing him back to life.

* * *

The party was in full swing and the guests were behaving themselves. Sophie couldn't help but feel proud that her first attempt at getting the Hungry Lion more business was a success. She scanned the crowd and smiled when Dave waved to her. He was dressed as a ship's Captain and giving orders to "his crew."

Sophie spotted one of their waitresses, who sported a bar wench's outfit. A customer was giving her a hard time, so Sophie signaled to one of the bouncers they had hired for the evening. He promptly went over and talked to the troublemaker. Sophie chuckled when the culprit apologized to the waitress.

With everything going smoothly, Sophie headed to the bar parched and a little hungry after hours on her Tinker Bell feet. Plus, she wanted to see Jake. He looked so handsome in his pirate suit. Her nerves danced, and her lips warmed at the memory of his kiss.

And there he was. All six-three of him. He slid a bottle of beer down the bar to a ready hand and winked at the woman who sat in front of him. But, Sophie saw something in his vigilant stance. An uneasiness. His eyes scrutinized the room as if looking for something—or was he waiting for something? She came up behind him and tapped his shoulder. His movements were quick and jerky to see who it was.

"You look like you need a break."

He bit his bottom lip and nodded. "Can you find someone?"

"Yeah, I'll be right back."

She found Dave across the room talking intimately to a woman dressed in a sleazy policewoman uniform. Their heads were close, eyes intense on one another. However, Dave's hand appeared clenched around her arm to secure her in place. At closer inspection, Sophie saw the stern look in his eyes and knew this wasn't some drunk trying to pick him up.

"Everything all right here?" Sophie questioned with caution.

"Yup. What's up?"

"Can you fill in for Jake? He needs a break."

"Is he okay?"

Dave's concern touched Sophie's heart. "I think the crowd is getting to him."

"Leave," he told the woman.

"This is a public place, and if I want to—"

"I don't give a rat's ass what you want. *Leave.*"

The woman sized Sophie up. "Do you think it's right how Dave is treating me?"

Dave stood in front of Sophie, successfully excluding her from the conversation. "She has nothing to say to you. Out, before I call the cops. And don't come back."

"Fine," she huffed then stormed away.

"Who was that?"

"None of your concern, Sophie," Dave said as he moved away and into the crowd.

"Wait a damn minute."

Anger edged every word when he turned back to her. "I said it's none of your business. Now drop it."

"Really?" Sophie crossed her arms. "I don't like being left in the dark, Dave."

"You're not. And I don't want it mentioned to Jake."

"Why?"

"Because I said so, okay?"

"Fine. But I don't like it."

"You don't have to."

Sophie rose to the tips of her toes to watch Dave move easily through the crowd. She then scanned the room to see if the mystery woman actually left, which she had. *Mild-mannered Dave lost his temper*, she mused. Most days the man seemed to be unshakable, but this unexpected encounter appeared more like an ex's attempt at reconciliation than an unruly customer who'd gotten under his skin. Finally, Dave tapped Jake's shoulder, and without hesitation Jake headed to the back room. A split second before disappearing, she saw him pull his hat off and run a hand through his hair.

"Hey Dave, can I have two waters?" Sophie yelled over the noise.

"Sure," he grumbled.

He planted them on the bar and Sophie started the adventure to her office. On the way she was stopped by a man who asked if her "twins" would like to go on a date. Then someone smacked her on the ass. When she turned to see the offender, no one looked guilty. Just shy of the office, she was cornered by two lesbians who asked her if a party concerning all three of them sounded like fun. Flattered but not interested, Sophie politely declined.

She opened the office door slowly. When she saw Jake sitting on the couch with his head in his hands, she came in and closed the door.

"Hey," she whispered, after kneeling in front of him with the waters in hand.

Peeking at her through the fingers covering his face, Jake said, "Was it that obvious I needed to get out of there?"

"No." She petted his hair down from where he ran his hands through it. "Only I could tell. I brought you some water." She held up the bottle and he smiled at her.

"Thank you."

"Too many people?"

"Yeah. From time to time, crowds get to me." He frowned. "Occupational hazard."

"Was it tough, doing what you did?"

His eyes were hard on hers, as if remembering what brought

on his claustrophobia also caused him pain. The first glimpse at his weakness reeled Sophie's mind back to Dave and their conversation.

"Jake…" she whispered, taking his face in her hands. "It's okay."

"No, Sophie. I don't think it ever will be. I'm a coward now."

"What?" *What do I do? What do I do?* The question repeated in her brain while she tried to think of reassuring words to give him.

"I closed the door in your face today because you scare the hell out of me."

She laughed a little despite his seriousness and her nervousness. "And you don't think you do that to me?"

"Please. I'm not a fool."

Sophie watched him gulp his water while she decided what next to say. How much did she really want to know about him, or have him know about her? "Jake, I'm not the same woman I was even six months ago. I was discouraged from taking risks, taught to always listen to my parents, and did what I was told by my lying, cheating asshole of a boyfriend. Hell, even my name doesn't fit me!" She took a deep breath before continuing. "My edges have always been a little rough despite relentless polishing. I never used to swear, and up until I socked you in the stomach, I haven't hit anyone since grammar school."

"Well, I'm glad to have been your first victim in a while," he told her dryly.

"What I'm trying to tell you is that I worked on myself a little at a time. When I was a child, my parents constantly had to reprimand me into behaving. They were so proud when I agreed to marry Bruce. Taking control of my life wasn't easy, Jake. When was the last time you just let go?"

Jake sat back on the couch, studying her. "So what you're sayin' is that I don't need to be in charge anymore?"

"Yes, Gunnery Sergeant. There're some things you can't control, so stop trying to and accept that things happen for a reason."

Jake looked away from her. She could see the agony on his face, and her heart became a little more his. "The last time I wasn't in control, I lost good men and got shot."

Sophie sat on the sofa next to him and pulled Jake into her arms. He moved toward her willingly, but she knew he still held back a part of himself—a fraction he quite possibly would never be able to let go of.

"I'm still so unsure of myself," she told him, "and yet I can put on this front of self-confidence in hopes no one will notice."

She felt his lips nuzzle her neck, and she closed her eyes.

"You'd never know, Sophie." He leaned her back onto the couch, covered her body with his, and touched her face. "I need to get back out there."

"We both do." Sophie's insides turned to liquid when he gave her an unmistakable look of barely controlled passion.

"Thanks for the water." Jake made no move to get up. Instead, he shifted a fraction and she felt the need she saw in his eyes.

"Anything else you're hungry for?"

"You're a wicked woman." He pressed his body into her and rubbed. She answered his call by wrapping her legs around him and pressing her lips to his throat.

With one hand, he pulled the front of her costume down while the other held her bottom in place so he could feel her.

"Damn it, I want you now."

Suddenly, she felt his mouth everywhere. She struggled for a breath but couldn't quite catch it with the passion they released in each other. His hand molded her breast while his tongue flicked the tip of her nipple. He suckled and stroked her skin, and his free hand slipped between her legs to tease her. At his touch, Sophie sensed she was losing perspective of the situation. With her hands on his shoulders, she tried to push him back. "Jake. Jake. We need to stop." He nipped at her breast, and she gripped his hair.

"I'm not letting you go," he told her.

"I don't think we're ready for this yet. I thought I was, but maybe we should learn a little more about each other first. You know, do the whole confession thing." Under him in a tangle of limbs and lust she felt Jake's body hesitate.

"This was just going to be sex," he told her and kissed her heated flesh. Sophie's body bowed in response.

"Yes, Jake. I wouldn't dream of destroying your reputation as the bar stud by tricking you into a relationship," she said, as her heart ached. He bit her not so gently on the shoulder, and she swatted him on the head. "Now that wasn't nice."

"I'm not always a nice man, Sophie." Jake rested his head against her chest while she stroked his back. Contented silence cradled them for a few precious moments. "Sophie, why am I so attracted to you?" He propped his chin on one hand and stared down at her. "You're slightly bitchy, physical when provoked not to mention, rebellious."

"Have you been talking to my parents? 'Cause that's just wrong. And you're confusing and pigheaded."

He grinned. "You're right. And for the record, so are you." He kissed her hard on the lips, and his hands began to wander. He then jumped off the couch and held out a hand to help her up. "Ready?"

"Ready? You half-undressed me. Teased me to distraction. And now you want to be nice?" She pushed off the sofa with a good-natured huff. When she saw him reach to touch her, she gave his hand a friendly smack.

"Oh, I'm sorry. Did I do to you what you've been doing to me for weeks?"

Frustrated, Sophie attempted to fix her hair and costume "And what is that?"

Crossing his arms while leaning toward her, Jake laughed. "Leave me feeling confused, unsure, and horny?"

She narrowed her eyes at him, then laughed, too. "Yeah! Exactly! You're confused and unsure if you want me, and I'm so tied up in sexual need that I think I'm going to have to start buying cases of batteries for my vibrator."

Jake pulled her into his arms, and something tender bloomed inside of her. With a gentle kiss, he told her, "Sophie, I'm going to make our first time more special than anything you've ever experienced. It means a lot that you're willing to be understanding about this."

"Jake, I'm going to rock your world." She began to fix the way his shirt hung over his broad chest. "We need to get back out there."

"Here, let me help you back into that costume." He placed his hands on her breasts and molded them together.

"That's not helping, Jake; that's teasing." Up on the tips of her toes, Sophie touched her lips to his. "When you're ready, I'll be too." But would her heart? It seemed he already owned more than half of it.

"I don't know what I did to deserve you, but I'm glad I did it. Now let's get out of here before Dave comes lookin' for us."

As they walked out to the party, hand in hand, Dave met them outside the office door. "I was just coming to check up on the two of you."

"All is good in the world," Sophie informed him.

Jake smacked Dave on the back. "And don't worry, little brother. I still have my innocence."

Sophie chuckled as she watched the brothers joke around. Something had changed. She couldn't describe it—the words simply eluded her. But she now understood that Jake's existence had just become vital to her happiness. And that frightening fact not only scared her, it made her smile with joy.

Chapter 7

In the weeks following the party, things progressed nicely. Sophie had an awesome girls' night out with Kathy, something they hadn't been able to do in months. They were finally able to talk about Jake and Dave. Kathy really seemed smitten with Dave, but due to her reserve, she refused to come back into the bar because she didn't want him to think she was stalking him. No amount of reassurance by Sophie would change her mind. Therefore, she decided to let fate take on the task of putting these two people together, if it was meant to be.

Bruce had stopped leaving messages on her cell phone. Sophie felt so relieved that she ran out to buy the most awesome pair of red high heels she ever saw. A genuine smile crossed her face when she looked over the expense report. Things were starting to turn around. Her parents even accepted the fact that she wasn't having a crisis of some kind, that she was a grown woman choosing her own career path.

Sophie sipped her morning coffee then swiveled her new office chair to the cabinet behind her. The expense report showed that within the months she worked for the Sanders brothers, the business had an upswing of ten percent. She couldn't help but feel proud as she filed the statement away. Of course, it was largely due to the Halloween party—but hey, it was only the beginning, and the holidays were just getting started.

She turned back to her desk, but saw the couch out of the corner of her eye. A grin crept across her face as she thought of her and Jake's steamy encounter. If she closed her eyes, Sophie could still feel his hands and lips on her. She wanted him in the worst way. He was dangerously gorgeous, and she would be fooling herself if she didn't take the sexual attraction between them into account. But, somehow in the last few weeks, her lust for him had become an essential yearning to talk, laugh, and simply be within his presence. Something about Jake brought out her softer side. A grace Sophie usually only possessed when dancing because of her parents' constant suffocation of her true character. With Jake she felt free to be who she was without worries of saying or doing the wrong thing. It even appeared that he enjoyed her occasional harsher edges.

She was then saddened by the knowledge that her parents would never approve of Jake. Her heart ached for their approval, just this once. No, he didn't have the country club breeding or the impeccable manners that never faltered even when challenged. Nope, none of that. Jake Sanders was a good man, plain and simple, and that was what mattered to her most. When she looked into his eyes, Sophie didn't see the voided stare of a man's true emotions gone UA, or Unauthorized Absence, as she found the Marines called it. Instead, she saw a man who would do anything for the people he loved, even if that meant keeping his distance. And that one fact, above all else, moved her heart in his direction. What would it be like to have him care for her like that? To know that he would do everything in his power to make sure she was safe and happy? Sophie never had anyone sacrifice it all for her before, and she wondered if, given the chance, Jake ever would.

The knock came first, then Dave stuck his head in. "Hey, you have some swanky-looking visitors here."

"You're kidding, right?"

"Nope." He gave her a hesitant smile. "I think they're your parents. I heard them talking to Jake."

"Now that's not funny, Dave." She studied his expression and soon realized he was serious. "Okay, I'll be out in a minute."

Sophie panicked and tried to find an escape route. There was always the window. She could fit through and make a run for it. *Naw.* That would leave Dave and Jake to deal with them. *Oh, Lord, Jake's out there with them!* The thought got Sophie to her feet and moving. She opened the office door hard enough to bang it against the back wall and echo out into the dining area. Sophie had always been known for her door-smashing ability.

They were sitting at the bar, and Jake was pouring her mother a glass of red wine. Sophie's father gave his balding head a frustrated rub with one hand as he held a beer bottle in the other. It gave her a sense of pride whenever she saw his small rebellions. Her mother always said drinks should be sipped from a proper glass, not guzzled from a bottle.

"Mother. Father." Sophie put out her hands to them and kissed both their cheeks. She tried to keep the strain out of her voice, but in vain.

Her mother smoothed her perfect chignon. "What in heaven's name did you do to your hair? Blond, Sophie? Really, you must get it fixed right away."

"I happen to like it, Mother. What are you doing here?"

"We wanted to see where our beautiful daughter has been hiding," her father said.

"I'm not hiding." Sophie worked her way behind the bar. She took the bottle of water and the wink Jake offered. "Thank you. Mother, Father, this is Jake Sanders. Jake, these are my parents, Nathanial and Antoinette Agnés."

Jake shook hands with both. "Nice to meet you. Your daughter's an incredible asset to our business."

"Why thank you, Jake." Antoinette turned to her daughter with a sharp eye. "We don't believe this is her true calling, but we will humor the idea until she decides to grow up."

"Okay," Jake drew out. "I think I'm going to step on some toes here, but—"

Sophie put a hand on Jake's bicep and shook her head. "It's all right."

Jake looked at her father and mother with disappointment then turned away. "I'll be in the kitchen checking the menu for tonight," he grumbled.

"Thanks, Jake." She watched him leave while her insides jumped with pure joy. *He was trying to protect me!* Wondering what he would have said to her parents if she hadn't stopped him Sophie turned to see some of the regulars nod at her as if to say, *Hey, we got your back.* It comforted her to know how accepted she was—even if they were eavesdropping.

Antoinette let out a long exasperated sigh while she smoothed the silky material of her pants. "I didn't mean to upset your friend. Is he the man who accompanied you to Bruce's? I must say, I can see why Bruce was so shaken after the two of you left."

"Jake didn't threaten him, if that's what you're insinuating."

"But his black eye!" her mother exclaimed.

"I told you, *I* gave it to him. Did Bruce tell you Jake did?" Loathing filled her and was about to boil over when her father reached a hand out and touched hers.

"We really are concerned for your welfare. Your mother and I don't want to see you having an affectionate—well, you know what I'm saying—with someone who is less than suitable."

The laughter came first from Stuart then hoots from Louie. Sophie turned to the men and winked when Louie shouted, "Gunny, Jake? Hit someone? He's a marshmallow. It's this little lady you need to look out for."

"Father, Mother, ignore them. And I'll say it again: Jake is not the one who hit Bruce. I am."

"I won't believe that," Antoinette stated with firm discontentment.

"Well, if our little girl clocked him good, then I'm sure he deserved it," Nathanial announced.

"He did," the deep voice behind Sophie said. "I'm Dave, Sophie's boss." He extended a hand. "My brother only went along to help move her things, but Brucie-Bruce had other ideas."

"Well, then, I'm glad Mr. Sanders was there. But, I still can't imagine what Bruce would have done to get such a violent reaction out of you. He was always so—"

"Mother, the man cheated on me and is moving into our summer home with his very pregnant girlfriend. He lies, and he was making every effort to get back into my bed so that the cash machine wouldn't be turned off. What is it you two don't get? I thought you both accepted this."

Nathaniel cleared his throat. "I don't know why you have to be so emotional all the time, dear. It's just that the two of you were together for so long."

Sophie turned to her father with venom in her eyes. She could feel their betrayal so potently that her hands began to shake from the toxicity. "Emotional?"

"Sophie," Jake's voice rang in her ear.

"Sweetheart, the only reason we came here was because we have tickets to the ballet next Saturday, and we wanted to know if you'd like to join us."

"And who will be my companion, Mother?"

Her father cleared his throat again, and looked at his wife. "Dear, under the circumstances, I don't think this is the right time."

"Yes, maybe you're right. Sophie, we will talk about this tonight, over supper."

When Sophie scoffed at them she felt Jake rubbing his hand up and down her arm. He began to do that more and more lately. Little touches, here and there, out in public where everyone could see. "I'm sorry Mr. and Mrs. Agnés. Sophie has the night shift tonight."

Nathanial gave Jake a sad father's smile. "Surely you won't mind if we take our daughter out? It's been well over a month since her mother and I have seen her."

"I think I would mind. Two people trying to convince my lady she should go to a ballet with her ex-fiancé? Yeah, I think I do mind. I also think Sophie would, too. Right?"

She was so proud of him. Jake saw through their ruse and still spoke with tact and respect. She really adored this man. Plus, he said she was his "lady." The sound of it had her smiling up at him.

"I'm sorry. We didn't realize Sophie began a relationship so soon after the breakup."

"Six months, Mother. That's not so soon. Why can't you accept this?"

"Well, I think we should be going. You can't blame your parents for wanting the best for their daughter."

Sophie growled, "He's not what's best for me. I wish you'd both see that."

Antoinette rose from her stool and handed Nathanial her long fur coat. He helped her into it without comment. Sophie sighed. The man was trained and turned into a bore by her mother. She reflected on how Nathaniel always said little, unless her mother was absent.

"We love you," Nathanial told Sophie. He then leaned over the counter and hugged her, then whispered in her ear, "I'm glad you punched him."

"Nathanial, please, it's not like we're never going to see her again." They walked out, but not before her father winked back at Sophie. He always was the one to save her, especially from her mother's displeasure.

"Wow."

She walked out from behind the bar and toward her office. "Ugh! They're insufferable. I can't believe they'd stoop so low!"

Jake followed her into the office just as Sophie started throwing things. He ducked as the pencil holder whizzed past his head. "What the hell! I'm not the one to blame here."

She felt marginally better after hearing the crash. "I like to throw things, okay? If you're in the way, then that's your problem." With that she threw a tissue box across the room.

"Fine. Just don't do it at my head. Remember? I'm the one who saved you out there."

"You did no such thing," she seethed.

"Really? I could call and let 'em know you really do have the night off."

"You wouldn't dare." She poked him with a finger, hoping to drill a hole right to his heart, then maybe she would finally know how he felt about her. Thoughts of him weighed heavy, a crushing pain that eased only when he offered strength and empathy. She didn't want to be the woman who needed reassurances of what a man felt for her. And yet, she found herself wanting that and so much more from Jake. Emotional assurances that her parents and Bruce never gave her: encouragement, affection, comfort in times of stress. Was that too much to ask? And did desiring these things make her pathetic and needy?

"No, I wouldn't," he told her, while taking the offending hand. "It would hurt you, and I would never do that." He kissed her palm, and Sophie softened at his touch, his show of tenderness.

"I'm sorry. I can be very difficult at times." She rolled up to the tips of her toes to give him a kiss, but Jake backed up. "What's wrong?"

"Last time we did that, we ended up on the couch."

"You could invite me over for dinner and we could be on *your* couch, for a change." Sophie rubbed her body against his and smiled when he let out a long whistle.

"God, you're a siren."

"I wouldn't want to deter you, but..." She kissed his neck and nipped at his earlobe. "I'm very much into bad movies and buttery popcorn, and I wouldn't mind necking on the couch."

He snickered at the invitation. "I think I can accommodate you...as long as you promise not to throw anything else at me."

"I promise."

Jake cupped her face in his hands and gave her a kiss so deep she felt it inside her soul. "Wanna order grinders or pick something up on the way there?" he asked.

"Whatever you want, it's yours."

However Sophie couldn't help wondering if she was talking about the food or her heart.

Chapter 8

Jake awoke drenched in sweat. Every muscle and nerve beat with an intensity too painful to comprehend. He lifted a hand in front of his face, but his fractured mind couldn't register the five-fingered appendage he saw. Confusion from a dizzying lack of understanding pulled him out of bed and into a fetal position on the floor. His grasp on reality slipped a little more as his body quaked. Jake felt the deep break in his psyche expand until the madness inside of it engorged the expanse of his mind. Crying out, he fought one last time for survival. Giving up was never an option. His duty was to always save lives and fight for the weak. But what if he'd become one of the defenseless?

Flashes of faceless people with images of incomprehensible injuries pulled Jake deeper into his own anguish. He clawed his way out of the damp, hollowed hell, feeling much like the night he became nearly inoperative within that grenade crater. Glaring light from the window beside him helped the nightmare fade, but the ramifications had become clear. His body was pasty, cold, and shaking from his wet skin. As his stomach lunged with a dry heave, Jake ran to the bathroom.

Disorientation muddled Jake's mind, making it almost impossible for him to distinguish between reality and the tricks his subconscious was playing on him. His vision was blurry, and the walls seemed to be moving in a fluid motion. When he tried to stand, his legs gave out, leaving him with the one feeling he hated most...helplessness. Not just because of his present condition, but because he knew it would be at least two days before he felt like himself again.

Slowly, Jake placed a hand on the bathroom sink and pulled himself up. In the mirror he saw a man in need. His eyes were swollen and his lip bled from biting it sometime during his nightmare. He avoided looking himself directly in the eye, for fear of what he might see, as he opened the cluttered medicine cabinet and took out some pills. He swore ripely when a few slipped down the sink drain because of his still-shaking hands.

"Damn it." Reluctantly he made eye contact with himself in the looking glass. "You need to get yourself together, buddy."

His mind and body exhausted from the war that raged inside his head, Jake dragged himself to the phone to call Dave.

"I'm not going to make it in," he told him.

"You okay?"

"Yeah. No. Haven't decided yet."

Concern coated Dave's voice, "Want me to send some food over?"

The thought of eating left Jake's stomach turning. "No, I have plenty here, thanks."

Jake hung up the phone without waiting for an answer. He knew Dave would worry but give him the space he needed.

"And this is why you probably shouldn't have a job," he mumbled to himself while turning on the shower taps. "You're certifiable."

The spray was a welcoming cleanse to the horrible night. As he leaned a hand on the shower wall to brace himself, Jake tried to remember aspects of the dream. Some were clear, others fuzzy. That was how they had been for the better part of two years. The therapist he had seen when he first got back from overseas said it was natural for the mind to block out what could be harmful to the conscious. Jake only wished he could remember everything so the dreams would stop. Or would they? The therapist also told him that wasn't always the case, because the nightmares varied from person to person and the degree of trauma they suffered. And boy had Jake suffered.

Jake went about his day uneasily. Shower, breakfast, two hundred pushups, talked to Dave when he called. Shower, lunch, run fifteen miles on the treadmill, talked to Dave because he called again. Shower, read, paced the floor for a few hours, then went outside and took a brisk walk. Only to come home to Dave calling, once more. Fed up, Jake demanded Dave to stop stalking him, because he was fine.

As the light faded outside his kitchen windows, Jake realized, with sudden sorrow and a frantic, beating heart, that he'd managed to successfully ignore his bedroom all day. Closing his eyes and taking a deep breath, he cursed the mayhem waiting for him and felt certain it could wait a little longer.

The living room clock chimed, announcing the six o'clock hour. Chicken and salad tonight for dinner, he decided while opening his pantry. It looked barren, so he decided he'd go shopping tomorrow. With the music blaring, he prepared his meal until the soldier inside him suddenly kicked in.

In half a heartbeat Jake pinned the intruder behind him on the floor with their hands behind their back and his knee pressed on the base of their neck. As his mind caught up to what he was doing, he saw a small-framed person lying underneath him. Jake began to panic. With slow and cautious movements he loosened his hold and removed his knee. A fist flew up and clocked him in the jaw. Then the feminine body sprang for the corner of the kitchen cabinets and huddled there.

"Oh shit! I'm so sorry." Jake moved toward Sophie, who tucked her knees up to her chest and wrapped her arms tightly around them.

"What the hell, Jake!" she yelled. After careful analysis Jake realized that while her body might have shown a frightened woman, Sophie's demeanor was as pissed as a caged wild cat. *And just as dangerous*, he thought while testing his jaw.

He crawled to her on his hands and knees. "I'm sorry. I didn't know it was you behind me. It was a gut reaction." Uncomfortable with the way she stared at him, Jake sat back on his haunches and brought his hands up to scrub his face. "There is no excuse. God, I didn't hurt you, did I? Please let me look to see if I bruised you."

As he reached for her, Jake prepared himself for Sophie to shrink away. But she didn't. Instead, she scooted forward and took him in her arms. That forgiving gesture nearly had him in tears.

"If you didn't have that awful music so high you would have heard me ringing the bell and pounding on the door."

"I'm so sorry." He buried his face in her sweet-scented hair and held tight to her understanding.

"It's okay, Jake. I'm okay," Sophie told him as she stroked his head and back.

Jake wasn't sure how okay he was. In such a short time she had become someone he wanted to talk and joke with. He looked forward to seeing her smile every day. The night before they shared a movie along with popcorn and kisses on his couch, Jake was able to see himself as a normal person. And when the temptation to go further presented itself, Sophie had popped off the sofa with a smile and said good night. Now he might have ruined that peaceful place they began building together.

Yet she held him close with no fear and blame. Jake thought about all the women who had come and gone in his life. None had ever made him feel so safe and loved. Even now, after scaring her, she talked to him in that sweet voice:

"You know, your brother warned me not to come here. But I never listened to my parents, so why the hell would I listen to him?"

He chuckled a little and pulled away to see her face. "Sophie, you're crazy."

"I know, and more than a little about you." She gave him a pensive smile then asked, "Are you okay? I was worried when Dave said you weren't coming in. What happened?"

He heard that right, didn't he? She was crazy about him? The realization only made his losing control that much more serious. Why did he always have to let down the ones he cared about? "Am *I* all right? Are *you* all right? I must have hurt you. Please, let me look," he pleaded, with self-loathing coating each word.

"Don't change the subject. I asked what happened."

"I'll confess my sins if you first let me see if I hurt you." When Sophie's mouth twitched in contemplation, Jake laughed, "I'll even let you stay for dinner. Okay?"

She stood before him and offered a hand to help him off the floor. "Fine. But don't think you're going to get out of this. I don't care what kind of military man you were. I want an explanation and I'll get it."

Jake took her hand and pulled her back down to him. When she fell on top of his chest, he rolled so she lay under him. "I want to see." He unbuttoned her blouse and began to kiss the delicate skin beneath it.

"Jake—"

"You hit the floor so hard." He rubbed his face against her chest. "I'm a monster," he mumbled against her breast, then kissed it.

"No, you're not."

With his index finger, Jake circled a small area on her collarbone. "I did hurt you." He heard his voice crack, and he assumed Sophie must have heard it, too, because she cupped his face and brought it to hers.

"I'm okay. And, I promise to stomp and grumble loudly whenever I think you don't know I'm there." She kissed him.

"I need to see." He rolled her onto her stomach then slid her shirt off. The deep red mark at the base of her neck almost did him in. The thought of standing in front of a firing squad was more appealing then facing this—the fact that he bruised her delicate, beautiful skin. Jake pressed his lips together as shame overcame him. Never had he laid violent hands on a woman before. Nor had he ever found someone to be as forgiving as this woman lying in front of him. "Why are you still talking to me? Sophie, I'm so sorry. I'll never touch you again." He rose to his feet and busied himself by pulling out lettuce from the fridge to chop with a vengeance. "I'll quit the bar, and you won't have to see me again."

"You self-absorbed ass! You think that's going to make things better?" she huffed, while yanking on her shirt.

"I think it's for the best," he mumbled. "What I did was inexcusable and—" He felt something hard hit his head. "Ouch! What the hell?" Turning in time to catch the wooden spoon that clocked him, Jake pulled it from her hands.

"I will not be dismissed," she yelled in fury while buttoning her blouse.

"What are you talking about?" he shouted.

"You think quitting the bar is going to stop what's happening between us? That that's the answer?"

"Yes, I do." Jake's body began to vibrate with frustration. How could he explain to her what she couldn't possibly understand? She would never stay with him, anyway; he was a lunatic.

"Why?"

"Because I obviously can't control myself. For Lord's sake, look at what I did to you!" He grabbed her arm and dragged her down the hall. His emotions were jumbled in a mess of madness, and the urge to learn to control himself became a nagging bitch on his shoulder.

"Jake, I will not be manhandled this way."

Fury had his blood roaring in his ears, pinpointed his sight on his directive. He lead her, none too nicely, into his bedroom where the sheets were torn and the blankets hurled to the ground. The night table lamps, smashed on the floor, were mixed with the feathers from his pillow. It all resembled debris from a battle. Glaring at it, Jake couldn't help but think of the room as a war zone—his own personal one. Yet, when he turned to face Sophie, the understanding in her eyes sent his rage into retreat.

"This is why I didn't come in today." His quiet voice reflected the defeat he felt inside. "I live with this every day, Sophie. I can't ask you to share it."

"You haven't, and I'm starting to think I'm just a nuisance that you're passing time with. Why won't you open up to me, Jake?" She faced him, a tear rolling down her cheek.

"Please don't do that," he pleaded.

"I can't help it. I know I'm not the easiest person to be around, but I truly care about you."

He pulled her into his compassionate arms and she went willingly, her turmoil finding a place of solace to settle and rest. "This has nothing to do with you being…" He pulled back and looked at her with a crooked grin. "You're not a difficult person at all. Sometimes you're too understanding and it gets me mad. Like right now."

"It wasn't your fault, Jake." Another tear escaped and Jake wiped it away.

"I care for you, Sophie. And just can't stand the thought of hurting you like I did in the kitchen or how I might in the future. I'm so tired."

"If you think you're tired now, wait until we're done cleaning up this mess." She kissed him softy and walked out of the room. "You making me dinner, or what?" she called out. "We're gonna need energy."

"Woman! You're a puzzle, a challenge, and a bossy little thing!"

"Well, it's not going to make itself."

* * *

She sat on his marble counter and wondered what she'd gotten herself into. She tried to be nonchalant, make a little joke, but her insides were shaking. No man had ever put his hands on her before. It might not have been in anger, but Jake scared her enough to rethink the relationship they were building and consider the ramifications of being involved with a man who suffered from PTSD. Sophie had told the truth when she said she understood what happened on the kitchen floor. It hadn't been his fault. If she'd listened to Dave in the first place, she might have saved Jake from the additional pain of what her surprise presence had caused him.

But here he was, staring at her intensely, longing swirling in his eyes. Sophie shifted on the countertop as a realization struck her: he was worth any struggle. It wasn't just his body she wanted, or his wicked sense of humor. No, this feeling went deeper than that. He filled the emotional emptiness she felt with a strong mental connection.

He cupped her face between his massive hands. Slowly their lips met, and the world evaporated. If she could feel this loved, this needed, for the rest of her life, she'd be happy forever. Behind her closed eyelids Sophie saw sparks of light burst into color. Beneath her skin, warmth spread throughout her body. When desire exploded, Sophie drove her hands into his hair and let the frenzy take them over. He responded immediately by wrapping her legs around his waist and pulling their bodies as close as two people could be. His hands raced over her while his lips became impatient and demanding.

She couldn't catch her breath. His passion overpowered her, and his need was so apparent Sophie could feel her own body fervently responding. He grasped her ass and crushed them even closer together. Without warning, Sophie pulled her mouth from his and cried out Jake's name. Taking a fistful of her hair, Jake brought her mouth back to his for one more long, hungry kiss before stepping away. Vibrating with pleasure, Sophie stared at him. "Jesus, Jake." She could feel herself panting as he did the same. The sheen of sweat on his skin gave Sophie the urge to lick and taste a bit more. Instead, she licked her own lips and tasted him there.

"I...don't know what to say. I'm not sure what came over me."

Jake's eyes were round with disbelief toward his actions. "First, I have you on the kitchen floor. Then I drag you to my bedroom, now I'm assaulting you in my kitchen, again." He pulled his hands through his messy hair and grinned, "I liked this better than the first two."

"Me, too. Come here." Sophie reached out. When Jake took her hand, she brought his body between her legs. "I think we're just running on wild emotions."

"Sophie, you're my guardian angel."

"Yeah, well, your protector needs food."

He placed his hands on her knees and squeezed. "I'm so sorry."

"I remember a time when you told me I apologize too much." She placed a hand on his bristled cheek. "We'll figure this out, Jake. I promise."

Jake nodded his head in agreement. "Do you like Chinese?"

"I love it."

"Okay. But you need to help me clean up the lettuce I started chopping first."

Sophie huffed, "Men. There's always a catch with everything."

Chapter 9

I want to know what happened." Dave leaned over and pushed the barbell down on Jake's chest.

"This isn't funny," Jake complained. "You're hurting me."

"No, I'm not. Now, what happened?"

Jake pushed the bar up with all his might and his brother with it. "I can bench-press you, Dave."

"So." Not giving up, Dave shifted his weight and pressed down more. "You're the little brother, now start acting like it." He sounded strained, but he kept trying to pin Jake.

"I haven't been little since I was ten." The barbell slowly sank back down toward Jake's chest, despite his best effort. "What do you want?"

"Sophie."

With that one word, Jake pushed Dave up and off of him. "What do you mean you want Sophie?" He dropped the bar in its rack as if it were a toothpick in a trash can.

Dave's hands flew up in defense. "That's not what I meant. Don't beat me! I only want to know what's happening between the two of you. Honest."

Jake laughed hard and loud. He held his side as his body convulsed. "You should see your face. It's white as a sheet."

"What? You're screwin' with me? Fuck you!" Dave shoved his brother in the chest with both hands.

"Couldn't help it." His laughter continued to bubble up. Dave abruptly left the room, and Jake followed him. "Dave, it was a joke!"

"Well, I didn't think it was funny. I thought you were going to go ape on me. Jesus, Jake."

Jake pressed his lips together as he watched Dave pace the locker room. His every step echoed off the blue-tiled walls. "It was a harmless joke, and you're just too wound tight to see it. What do you want to know?"

Dave turned and looked at him. Jake couldn't be sure what mix of emotions he saw in his brother's eyes, but he knew love and understanding were among them.

"Are you sleeping with her?"

"No. And I can guarantee you'll be the first to know when it happens. I'll call right away."

Dave shook his head. "I'm serious. You in love with her?"

"Not sure. Again, you'll be the first to know."

"Have you told her about the flashbacks?"

Jake sat down hard on the worn wooden bench and began peeling his shoes and socks off. "She showed up after the last one a few days ago."

"What do you mean, Jake? What happened? How come you haven't told me about this?"

"Because I knew this is how you'd be. All protective and shit."

"I have a right to be that way. What happened?"

"She came up behind me and I reacted."

"Oh, no."

Jake pinched the bridge of his nose to ward off some of the tension. "Yeah. Then we went out for Chinese."

"Is that how she hurt her shoulder?"

Jake stopped in the middle of stripping his shirt off. "What are you talking about?"

"Her shoulder, Jake. She has a hell of a bruise and she's been babying it." Dave looked pensive for a minute then said, "Maybe you should go back to counseling. There's no shame in it."

Anger coursed through Jake's veins. He didn't want to go back, he wanted to move forward. "I'm working on it, Dave. And she said she was okay, damn it." He dropped his head in his hands. "Why can't I just be normal?"

Dave plopped on the bench beside his brother. "Because you never were. As a kid you always caught on faster and were better at everything. There were never boundaries for you. You excelled at school, sports, girls, and the military. Damn, bro. You were the youngest man to ever earn your rank. That says something. But there're boundaries now, and you need to learn them."

"If I was so great at everything, then why are you always right?"

"'Cause I'm the big brother."

"Dave, I think she might be the one." Jake shook his head in disbelief. "She didn't get angry with me, she didn't push to find out why I'm this way. She just understood it's who I am."

"It takes a special woman to put up with a military man. Especially one with baggage."

Jake huffed, "I have a lot of that, and it doesn't feel right to share it with her."

Dave put a brotherly hand on Jake's back. "She doesn't seem the type to give you a choice. By the way, Mom and Dad are coming in next week. They didn't want me to tell you, but seeing you're not very good with surprises…" Dave gave him a weak smile.

"No, I guess I'm not. I'm really starting to care about her, Dave."

"I know. I think she'll be good for you. I'm worried, though. She doesn't know how to deal with your 'needs,'" Dave said with air quotes. "Maybe, and only if you're serious about her, she can come to some support meetings with me."

"My temper isn't the problem anymore, Dave."

"I know that."

"It's my gut reaction, and I'm workin' on it. I feel more normal now than I have in a long time. I'm actually feeling things, not just looking for signs from others to know how I'm supposed to react." He knew what his brother was trying to say, ever so delicately. Hell, the guy had a right to be worried. Jake hadn't been home and out of the hospital for two months when Dave came up behind him. He'd broken Dave's nose and fractured his left arm before he'd gotten control of himself.

Back then Jake's brain had skipped and jumped. He would react at the wrong times and with too much force. After a year of therapy, he was more controlled than he'd ever imagined. Nevertheless, he wanted more. Jake sought to feel normal, and he was starting to realize it might be possible.

"No one says that you're not gettin' better. Hell, you worked the bar during that Halloween party with all those people. I wasn't sure how you were going to react to that, but you made it through. I'm proud of you." Dave took a deep breath and seemed to choose his next words carefully, "But are you ready for this relationship? There's still a lot you don't remember. It's a big step of trust, Jake."

Jake watched his brother pull a shirt over his head. The man didn't have a scratch on his tattooed body—unlike Jake's, which looked defaced in some areas. Silent disfigurements to remind him of another life he once believed in so strongly that he never questioned his own mortality. "Sophie showed up at the wrong time, on the wrong day," he finally said. "I don't want to hurt her. And knowing that I did…I don't know, Dave. Should I just forget about her?"

Dave snorted, "Yeah right, like she's going to let that happen."

"She's a hell of a woman."

"Yup. You were damn lucky she didn't strike back."

Jake snickered and pulled a fresh shirt over his head. "She hit me over the head with a wooden spoon."

Dave laughed, "You know, I like her. If it doesn't work out between the two of you, can I have a shot?"

"You lookin' for a death wish?"

"Actually, I'm looking for a beer. What do you say? Celebrate?"

"Celebrate what?"

Dave gave his little brother a small push. "You might be losing your virginity soon."

"You're an asshole."

* * *

"I don't know, Kathy. You really think I should?"

With cool eyes, Kathy scanned Sophie's downstairs ballet studio. "Sophie, you have a lot of talent, that's not the question. Why not share it?"

"Because then my mother is going to try and get involved."

"Please don't take this the wrong way, but why is your mother so…"

Sophie added in the words which Kathy didn't want to say. "Bossy, overbearing, mentally absent?"

"Umm, yeah. Was she an abused child, or something?"

Sophie let out a long breath before answering, "I don't know. I've never heard anything like that. You'd think with how she is there'd be something. Aside from the women in my family playing the weak-and-meek card, there's nothing."

"Well, she's not weak or meek."

"No, my mother isn't." Sophie did a quick pirouette for the hell of it. "Maybe if we understood each other better, we could have a real relationship. I don't ever see that happening, though."

"I love watching you dance. I have the grace of a rhinoceros."

"You just don't have quick feet."

"Thanks for trying to make me feel better, but the truth is the truth."

The girls smiled at one another, and Sophie thought about how special their childhood friendship was. They shared everything, and nothing was off-limits to talk about . . . except for what happened with Jake. Sophie still couldn't bring herself to discuss it. Kathy might not understand, and Sophie didn't want her friend judging Jake before meeting him. Besides, Sophie didn't totally understand herself. She needed time to process and decide exactly what she wanted. Unfortunately, all her thoughts kept going back to needing Jake.

"Sophie? You okay?"

"Sorry, Kathy. There're a few things on my mind."

"Do they have to do with a certain man?"

Sophie gave her a sly smile. "Maybe. You would have met him if you'd come to the Halloween party."

"I was visiting my brother," Kathy said with a wistful look in her eyes. "I love his kids."

"And someday you'll have a brood of them."

"Yup, and they all will learn ballet from one of the best when she stops being stubborn and opens the studio."

Sophie studied the room surrounding her. She took in the feel of it, the vastness of the space, the mirrored walls, and the long barre waiting for legs to be stretched on them. "It's not time yet."

Chapter 10

The chairs were comfortable enough, and most of the people seemed friendly. And yet Jake still wasn't sure if he belonged in what he termed "crazy class" instead of group therapy. Asking for help seemed to feel like a weakness. He'd been trained to take charge, follow orders, and put feelings and fears aside until the time came to deal with them. But after talking with Dave at the gym, Jake decided now seemed to be the right time to manage the baggage he'd successfully packed and hidden away. Besides, what did he have to lose?

None of the faces were familiar, but they all wore the same blank, bottomless expressions. He knew that look. It was the *I can't believe I'm doing this—I'm stronger than this* look. Watching a man across the circle from him, Jake not only saw but felt the vile anger he prominently displayed with the way he was sitting. His arms were crossed tight as he slouched in his chair and stared at a spot above everyone's head. Yes, Jake knew; he'd worn that look himself more than once.

"Okay, we're going to go around the room, introduce ourselves, and say what we're going to work on today," the director said. "Who's going to go first?"

Everyone either looked down or averted their eyes to avoid the imminent task.

"I'll go," the woman next to Jake said. "I'm Trisha, and I want to learn how to deal with my anxiety better." She then looked at Jake. He felt a small bead of sweat roll down his back as he pressed his hands firmly together. All eyes were on him. His heart beat so hard he wondered why everyone in the room didn't see it pulsing in his chest.

"I'm Jake and I want to work on post-traumatic stress." *Well, that wasn't too bad*, Jake decided as the man sitting on his other side spoke. *Like riding a bike.*

After introductions, the group broke for ten minutes, then they separated into smaller clusters for dependency abuse or emotional support. Following his need to help, Jake walked to the irritated man who still sat across from him.

"Hey," he said.

"What?"

Taken back by the quick response, Jake tried another tactic. "Not too happy about being here, are ya?"

With venomous eyes, the man turned and faced Jake. "Really? You can tell? I didn't think anyone would notice."

"Guess I just have good instincts."

"Well, if you did, you wouldn't have crossed the room to talk to me." The man stood and walked away. Then, with a huff, he sat in a chair away from everyone.

"That's Doc Murphy," Trisha told Jake. "He served in Afghanistan. Not a real friendly sort. Think he saw too much."

"I think we all saw too much if we're here," Jake said with a weary smile.

His new friend gave a little laugh. "Isn't that the truth?"

When break ended, the soldiers sat in a small circle to talk about how they were going to meet their goals for the day. Jake took the chair next to Doc Murphy, who slumped away from him.

Listening and watching his comrades was heartbreaking. Marriages failing, lack of trust, financial ruin, anger without a true understanding of where it came from, fear of failure. Jake slowly came to understand he should've come back sooner. As much as he'd felt the ceiling and walls were going to cave in or everyone would look at him as if he were the lunatic of the year, Jake now realized that wasn't the case. Some of these people were much worse off than he was. They didn't just struggle from day to day; they raged with war every minute. There was talk of taking their own lives, of hiding in their homes for days, living on the streets for years at a time, and being in jail. Jake had forgotten how lucky he'd been to have a supportive family and a somewhat sound mind. Then there was the fact that he wanted to start a relationship. A truly big step in his recovery. It showed trust—on his behalf and in her.

"Jake, you're not saying much. What's on your mind?"

He looked at the group leader. "I guess I'm still wondering if I belong."

"You asked for help, so you belong." When the group agreed, Jake took a deep breath and prepared himself to talk. He sat with his comrades, the only people who would truly understand his plight.

"Well, I'm having a hard time controlling my instincts." Doc scoffed, but Jake ignored him. "I want to get on with my life… but what if I can't? My parents are coming up to visit and I… I hate disappointing them."

"Oh, I know that feeling," someone said.

"That's why you're here, Jake. To learn the skills needed to function positively. Why do you feel as if you've disappointed your parents?"

"I've let a lot of people down. I'm a soldier. Always will be." He took a deep breath then looked at Doc Murphy. "But, how can I live with what I've done, seen, and can't remember?"

Doc looked at him, the pain intense in his eyes. "When you figure it out, let me know."

The rest of the meeting went well. When Jake emerged into the sunlit afternoon, he wasn't only feeling tired from the emotional morning; he also felt a little lighter. As if a giant weight had been lifted from his shoulders.

* * *

"So, how'd your first day go?" Dave swung his legs up on Jake's kitchen table. Jake pushed them down.

"Feet off my furniture. It went. Maybe I'm not as whacked out as you think."

"Oh no, you are. We just really like you, is all."

Jake watched his brother throw back a can of soda. The man was his rock, and it occurred to Jake he might never have told him.

"Dave…"

"God! Don't get all sloppy on me, Jake. My manhood might not be able to handle it. I'm the big brother, and I'm supposed to take care of you. Besides, you've had to kick my ass a time or two."

"Thank you. That's all I was gonna say."

Dave nodded at him in acceptance.

"Okay, 'big brother,' what do we want to order tonight?"

"How often are you going to the meetings?"

Jake looked up from searching through the box of menus. Dave wanted to talk, after all, and Jake found himself ready to do it. "Three or four times a week."

"What about your OCD?"

"Well...I guess we'll work on my compulsions, too. I think I'll start with not picking up my socks tomorrow morning."

Dave waved his hands in the air, "Don't get all wild on us, Jake!"

"Wait until I don't have all my TV remotes put away properly."

"Now that's just crazy talk. You obviously need to be committed."

"What do you feel like eating?"

"Italian. Meet any new friends?"

Jake pulled out a few menus and handed them over. "Yeah. There's a guy who's hell-bent on not talking."

"I'll have the veal parmesan. Boy, doesn't that sounds like someone I know."

"He told me to leave him alone." Jake snatched the paper out of Dave's hands. "I'm going to have the eggplant."

"Order some soda, too. Are you going to bug the crap out of him?"

"You've had enough soda, Dave. Yup, I'm going to work at him a little every day."

"I like soda, and you don't have any beer. Is that going to get in the way of your recovery?"

"There's iced tea and milk in the fridge. Too much soda is going to eat your stomach away. No, I'm going to keep talking to him until he slaps a restraining order on me."

"Fine. But next time you better have lemonade. The creeper routine always works with the ladies, too, you know."

"Ha ha. Now, let me make the call." Jake no sooner finished placing the order when Dave started in again.

"You gonna tell Sophie about this?"

"I'm not sure yet. When I was going last time, I had a lot of flashbacks and stuff."

"So you might have to. I think it'd be a good thing to do, since she's already seen what can happen."

Jake couldn't help frowning. "Yeah," he said quietly.

"I didn't mean to upset you, Jake."

"You didn't. It's just that you're right, and I hate that." He smiled at his brother so Dave would know there were no hard feelings. While Dave might have taken care of him in the past, it now was Jake's job to get Dave to stand down a little. Reassure him that everything was okay. Dave could be pushy and a little intrusive when it came to Jake's recovery. Then again, if Dave hadn't been, would Jake be where he was today—feeling pretty darn good?

"Jake. You gonna tell Mom and Dad when they get in tomorrow?"

"Stop with all the questions. I feel like I'm being interrogated."

"That's because you are. Answer the question."

Jake rolled his eyes. "No. I want them to enjoy their visit."

"And you think by not telling them that they aren't going to worry?"

Jake narrowed his eyes at his brother. "You already told them. Didn't you?"

"Yup, but they want to hear it from you."

"Dave, I know you're looking out for me, but—"

"Yeah, yeah, yeah," Dave interrupted. "I know it should have been you to tell them, but I knew you'd chicken out and they'd be worried the whole time they were here. I did you a favor, so say thank you."

It was always hard to be mad at Dave when he was only looking out for him. Now with the pressure off of Jake, and with his parents having had time to process his news, he hoped they wouldn't hover over him as much during their visit.

"Okay. Thank you, Dave."

"You're welcome. Now, let's go over the birds and the bees so you don't look like an inexperienced virgin when you decide to have fun with Sophie."

"Don't worry. I've been reading a lot of *Playboy* lately."

* * *

"I know, I know, I know!" Sophie tucked her legs beneath her on the couch. In the past few weeks she and Kathy had spent an enormous amount of time together. Not that Sophie would ever complain about Kathy taking time to travel while being laid off, but she'd missed her friend. It was nice to have her around to talk to. Sophie just felt guilty for not broaching the subject of Jake's flashback, and her nerves were beginning to dance from wondering what her friend was going to think.

"You're really falling for him, aren't you?" Kathy took a mouth full of peanut butter and chocolate ice cream.

"Yes, I think I am," Sophie told her friend with a wistful sigh. "He's so…"

"Hot?"

"Oh, yes!"

"Physically able to please a woman?"

"I believe so."

"Makes you laugh?"

Sophie smirked. "He called me bitchy."

"Well, it sounds like he already knows you really well. So, what's the problem?"

Sophie decided the hell with caution. She needed real advice from the only person she truly trusted. "You know those bruises on me?"

Kathy slowly put her spoon in her bowl. "Don't tell me he did that. You deserve better, Sophie. You, of all people, can't stand the whole 'helpless female' thing."

"Let me explain—"

"You're sticking up for the guy?" The shock on Kathy's face was as evident as her anger when she slammed down her bowl on the coffee table.

"He has flashbacks from the war, Kathy. I can't blame him for something Dave told me not to do."

"And that was?"

"Go over to his house unannounced. Dave said Jake wasn't feeling well, and I got concerned. Thought I could make him some soup or something."

"What happened?"

"He didn't hear me come up behind him. Before I knew what happened…" Sophie took a cleansing breath. "I was on the floor with my hands behind me and a knee in my back."

"Jesus, Sophie! Then what happened?"

"He must have realized it was me because he let go and I clocked him in the face."

Kathy snickered. "That's what? Three strikes in the past month? Maybe *you're* the one with issues."

"It's not something to be proud of. But all the parties and events involved deserved it."

"Okay, so he didn't hear you. I don't know, sweetie. I think you're going to have to really think about this. There seems to be some serious baggage here."

"Some? I think he has a trailer full. The thing is, I want to get to know him, understand what he's been through, and be there for support. I can't explain this pull we have toward one another. Am I crazy?"

"No. But he might be." Kathy gave Sophie's leg a playful slap. "Just joking."

"Ha ha." Sophie took a spoonful of her own ice cream and concentrated on what to say next. "He really felt bad, Kathy. I mean to the point where he was going to quit the Hungry Lion so I'd never have to see him again. He looked like he was going to cry, then he wouldn't stop apologizing. He even insisted on making sure I wasn't hurt by checking for bruises. I think if he knew my arms have been aching, he'd never forgive himself. What kind of man would go to lengths like that if he's an abuser?"

"Not the typical ones. I'm not saying he is, and I'm not saying that you shouldn't date him. It's just…well, is he getting counseling for his anger?"

Sophie began to pick at a thread on her sweater. "I honestly don't know. And, I don't think what happened had anything to do with anger. I think it was a gut reaction he couldn't help."

"So what are you going to do?"

"I don't know," Sophie exclaimed.

"Okay, how much do you like him?"

"So much it's been killing me. I mean he really is special. You should have seen the way he handled my parents. I've never had someone stick up for me when it came to them."

"Well, that's major bonus points in my book."

They looked at each other in silence, neither knowing what more to say to the other. Finally, Kathy spoke. "I think you should go for it. If he really didn't hurt you out of anger, and he's a standup guy when it comes to protecting you, then don't let him go. But I think you should be cautious, find out if he's getting help."

"I'll ask Dave tomorrow."

"You think that's all right? Jake might be a little ticked off by you going to his brother rather than him."

"Do you think I should wait 'til Jake says something to me? Dave already told me if there's something I wanted to know, to ask." Sophie was torn. She didn't want it to look as if she snuck behind Jake's back to find stuff out, but what guarantee did she have that Jake would talk to her? He'd been so tight-lipped about his past. Confused, Sophie covered her face with her hands. "I heard Dave saying their parents are coming in tomorrow. I'm nervous."

Kathy waved her off. "Really? Just let your inner bitch come out and they'll love you. And don't wait for him to come tell you because he might not."

"I know." Sophie chewed on her bottom lip. Why did this have to be so complicated? "I'll wait until his parents leave or he somehow opens the door."

"I think that's a good plan. Meanwhile, what do you think his assets are like?" Kathy sat up straight and leaned forward in anticipation of juicy details. "After all, I might someday date his brother."

"You're so bad, Kathy. No wonder my parents don't like you."

"And you do."

Sophie studied her friend for a minute, "Wait a minute... 'Might someday date his brother'?"

"Didn't miss that, did ya?"

"No. Kathy, is there something you're not telling me?"

"I don't know if there is anything to tell. Dave and I ran into each other yesterday at the supermarket."

The faint blush on Kathy's cheeks told Sophie there was more. "And...?"

"And, we talked... a little."

"About?"

"Oh, I don't know. Stuff."

"Like? I shouldn't have to pull this out of you. You're supposed to tell me everything."

"He asked for my number." Kathy gave a little squeal. "I think he's going to call me."

Sophie sat back on the couch and stared at her friend. She'd never seen Kathy so excited or nervous. "Are you going to answer if he calls?"

"Of course! I don't want to seem too eager, though."

Sophie laughed at her friend. "I think you have a real crush on him."

Kathy's chin shot in the air. "I do not. We just met."

"I know. That's what makes it sooooo sweet."

"We're off the subject, Sophie."

Sophie giggled and took a bite of ice cream. It was nice to have a friend when the world seemed to have abandoned her. "What do you want to know?"

"Everything. Now tell me."

"He's going to be a tight fit," Sophie said and wiggled her eyebrows.

"What? No way! So unfair! I haven't had something like that in…ever. How do you know?"

"Oh, we've had a little fun, here and there, and I got a good feel in." Sophie licked her lips. "I can't wait to get a hold of him. Literally."

"You're going to tell me every detail, Sophie. I'm not kidding. Every one. Or our friendship is over, because right now I'm living vicariously through you."

"I thought you were dating some guy named Sam?"

Kathy shrugged her shoulders. "We went on a few dates, and I wasn't feeling it for him. He was devastated."

"Well, yeah he was. You probably crushed him."

"I wouldn't say that. But he was a terrible kisser. I wish I was brave enough to walk up to Dave and smooch him good."

"Jake's an awesome kisser."

"And, that's why you have to tell me everything."

"I'll tell as much as I can."

"Promise?"

"Promise. Now, let's watch that movie. My ice cream is starting to melt."

Chapter 11

You really need more of a woman's touch in here." Renee looked around the Hungry Lion with a smile.

"Mom, you're never happy unless there's wallpaper everywhere." Dave passed his father an afternoon beer, and then laughed when his mother gave scowled at him.

"You know I don't like him to drink this early," she said.

"Honey, it's not the end of the world if I have a beer with my two sons," George replied.

"Fine," she sniffed. "Give me a dirty martini and make it strong." She parked her rounded rump on a stool and smiled. "I've missed you boys so much!"

"We've missed you too, Mom." Jake kissed his mother's cheek and shook the mixture before pouring it into a chilled glass for her.

"Don't lie to your mother, Jake. It's not nice to do, and you'll go to Hell for it."

"I'm not lying, Dad. I do miss you guys. When are you going to move back?"

Renee coughed into her drink. "Honestly, why would we move back to this frozen snowball? I love Florida."

"Your mother has never liked New England, boys. Me neither, now that I can play golf all year around." The older couple smiled at each other and then kissed.

Dave pretended to gag. "*Yuck*. Do you really have to do that in front of us?"

Renee sent her boys a mischievous grin. "Want to know what we do in the hot tub?"

"No!" they yelled in unison.

"Why do you both consistently try to embarrass us?" Jake rolled his eyes to the ceiling. "I mean really, that was gross."

Renee waved her son off. "Oh, you're too uptight."

"So." George shifted in his seat and looked Jake square in the eye. "Who's this new ladyfriend we're hearing so much about?"

"Thanks, Dave." Jake gave his brother a mild stare.

"No problem."

"We've only been on a couple dates. You'll like her. She's feisty." Jake couldn't cover the smile on his face. Sophie was more than feisty; she was a hellcat, and one he'd seriously been thinking about taking to bed. Everything about her called to his libido. He could remember a time when making a girl beg for more was his favorite pastime. Thoughts of wild nights, silk bondage ties, strawberries, and endless hours of making love slowly began to surface. If he ever let go and took Sophie, there would be nights they both would remember, forever. He'd take her in every way possible, driving himself into her while she held him with those long dancer's legs wrapped tight around his waist. Of course, he'd have to be careful. He was a big man, and not just in stature. More than once he'd been too big to fit. And while it was disappointing at the time, the thought did wonders for a man's ego.

Jake crashed back to reality when his father reached over the bar and hit his arm. "You all right, son? Kinda went on a small trip there."

"He's been like this for at least a month, Dad."

"I have not, Dave."

"My little brother here might be losing his virginity soon." Dave put his arm around Jake's shoulder.

Jake shrugged him off. "You're closer to a virgin than me."

"Who's a virgin?" The sweet sound of her voice made Jake's ears turn red.

"Not one of us," George answered, getting to his feet. "I'm George and this is my pain-in-the-ass wife, Renee."

Renee finished her drink and stood to shake hands. "And you are?"

Sophie stood staring at them for what seemed like an eternity. "I'm sorry. I'm trying to place you. We've met before."

Renee smiled. "Actually, George and I aren't only here to see our dimwitted sons. The truth is we wanted to meet you again."

Jake came from around the bar to stand next to Sophie. "You've met before? Where?"

Sophie smiled, "I'll have to honor you with a tour de force." She backed up to a clearing in the room. With her chin turned up and her expression serious, Sophie lifted one of her legs up behind her, the knee bent at a ninety-degree angle. It was turned well out, so her knee became higher than her foot. Jake couldn't help but wonder how she did it. Her arm on theside of the raised leg washeld gracefully over her head in a curved position, while her other arm extended to the side. Then Sophie began to spin. As her body whirled around and around her lovely face successfully paused in the exact position it started in. Jake heard his parents and brother cheer, but he was too flabbergasted to do anything but stare. When she came to a stop, he sat down on a bar stool. His parents rushed to her, talking wildly about how they'd enjoyed her performance at the Metropolitan Opera in D.C. two years ago.

Dave put a hand on Jake's shoulder. "What the hell is she doing here with us?"

"I don't know." Dumbfounded, Jake smiled when Sophie looked his way. But he saw no joy in her eyes for what she'd done. No breathlessness from a job well executed. He remembered the night they closed up after the Halloween party. She jabbered on and on about how great it had gone. How all the hard work was worth what they'd accomplished. He realized, with a sudden clarity, dancing came too easy for her. She was a natural with no passion—at least, not anymore.

"Oh, Jake! You are among royalty and don't even know it," his mother proclaimed.

"Trust me, I know, Mom." He took a swig of his water and winked at Sophie. "Would you like me to be your bouncer? My mom and dad are never going to leave you alone." He felt relieved when Sophie's laugh reached her eyes. He liked that a lot better.

"No, Jake. I think I'm okay with these crazy fans." She gave them each a hug and then took Jake's water for a sip. "What's on the books for today?"

"Just another day watching you try to organize the place." When they stared too long into each other's eyes, Renee cleared her throat.

"Why don't you dance anymore, Sophie?"

George shot his wife a warning look. "Babe, I think that's a personal question."

"It's okay. I dance for myself, now."

"Have you ever thought of teaching?"

"Renee, I've seriously thought about it," Sophie began, "but I don't enjoy it enough to teach. Without adequate passion, you can't get others excited."

Renee nodded as if to say she understood. "Jake's much the same."

"Okay, Mom. No need to drag me into it. I'm off to start working." He popped off his stool and headed to the backroom.

On the way, he heard his mother say, "Jake was training to be part of the secret service, you know. He was the best at what he did."

Jake closed the office door behind him. Maybe he shouldn't have walked away. It was a little bit childish. However, when his mother started talking about his past career, it made him uneasy. No, he didn't miss it. And his mother seemed to have a hard time understanding that. Jake liked who and where he was now, even if he was a little messed up. He flicked on the computer and rested his feet on the desk, crossed at the ankles. When the door opened, he wasn't surprised to see Sophie.

"So you were a big bad Marine." She sashayed toward him, while running a finger along the top of the desk. Jake saw mischief in her eyes, and he decided playing a little at work wouldn't be so bad.

"You have no idea." He ran a hand up her side to cup her breast. When his thumb grazed her nipple, she let out a ragged breath. "You're so beautiful." Bringing his feet down, he pulled Sophie on his lap. She went willingly, laughing.

"Mr. Sanders, I don't think this is a good idea."

"Probably not." He tugged her shirt up and started nibbling on the delicate skin between her breasts.

"Your parents are outside the door," she whispered.

"It makes this so much naughtier." He brought his mouth to hers and let the eagerness he felt for her rule. "I'll never get tired of touching you, Sophie."

"Jake." She leaned slightly away from him. "What has gotten into you? It wasn't that long ago you slammed a door in my face."

"It wasn't that long ago I had you turned into a puddle on my kitchen counter, either." He smiled wickedly at her. "I can't help wondering what it would be like if we did that without our clothes on." With one hand holding her neck and the other wrapped around her waist, Jake trapped her body with his.

"I have to get to work," she said against his lips.

"I need to feel you, only you. I've been up at night thinking about your lips on me. What they would do to me."

Her eyes grew wide at his suggestive comment. "Your parents are right out there. You're crazy if you think I'm giving you a blowjob here."

He smirked at her, mostly because he wanted to see her reaction. "No sense of adventure." When she narrowed her eyes at him, Jake discovered Sophie wasn't one to back down from a challenge, and he found that fact stimulating.

"Okay, big boy." She rose off his lap and proceeded to lock her office door. When he opened his mouth to object she said, "What's the matter? Afraid of getting caught with your pants down?"

"No. I'm a grown man."

"Let's see how much you can grow." She sank to her knees in front of him. Jake decided she was either bluffing really well or he was going to get the best oral pleasure of his life. When she carefully lowered his zipper, Jake knew it was the latter.

"It's been a really long time."

Sophie looked up at him and licked her lips, "I hope you're not a loud moaner." She released him from his restrictive boxers and slowly began to stroke him. "Wow, Jake."

He sucked in a breath when her tongue teased the tip. "Jesus,

Sophie. Maybe you were right. We really shouldn't be doing this." His hands gripped hard on the arms of the office chair as desire scorched through his body. When she took him into her mouth, Jake's head fell back and his hips pressed gently toward her.

"You need to make this fast, Jake." She smiled before licking up and around his shaft. Her tongue, her mouth, the suction, made him delirious with need.

She moved fast. Pumping and tasting him. She cupped his balls and Jake felt his eyes roll. His hands held fast in her hair and he pushed to the back of her throat. When she moaned, he bit his bottom lip hard to stop from making any noise. In a lust-filled daze Jake almost slid out of the chair to the floor.

He flung his hand to one side and knocked a pile of papers to the floor. As her speed increased to a fanatic level, Jake took a handful of her hair to keep her still while his muscles constricted and released. Sweat rolled down his face, and his body relaxed with euphoria. When he looked down he saw a wicked woman staring back at him.

"See what can happen when you lose control? I made you into a horny mess."

"Dear God, you're awesome." He lunged forward and fused his mouth to hers before they fell to the carpet. When the knock came at the door, they both began to laugh.

"Hey! Your father and I are leaving. I hope you're not too mad at me."

"I'm not," Jake yelled to his mother through the closed door. When Renee tried the doorknob, he winked at Sophie. "I'll be out in a minute, Mom. Sophie's been teaching me a lesson on personal motivation. Apparently, she thinks I've been lacking in that area." He covered Sophie's mouth to stop her giggles. Her eyes crinkled as she tried to hold back.

"Well, I would absolutely say so."

As they heard his mother walking away, Jake told Sophie, "She knows."

"What? How could she?"

He tilted his head and smiled down at her. "I feel great," he drew out.

"Good for you. Now get off of me, you big oaf," she laughed and pushed at him.

"I thought I was a 'Big Boy.'"

"Don't make me regret saying that. And right now you're an oaf stopping me from brushing my teeth and working. Stop smiling!"

"I can't help it. You're such a moody thing." He felt her hand a little too late. Jake hollered out when she twisted his nipple.

"Now get off of me," she giggled.

"Geez, you don't have to be so mean."

Sophie surprised him by wrapping her arms around the back of his neck and kissing him. "I'm glad you feel better. I know what your mother was talking to me about bothered you."

"I saw that you really didn't enjoy that show of your talent. Thank you for doing it for them." Jake rested his forehead to hers. "I think I'm falling for you, Sophie Agnés."

"I think you're talking with the wrong head right now." She giggled when he tickled her side. "Okay, okay. I like you, too."

He got to his feet then offered her a hand up. "How about supper tonight?"

"No."

She stood before him and Jake couldn't help the filthy thoughts he experienced while fixing his jeans. He wanted her naked and screaming his name. "I better clean up. Otherwise, more things will get knocked off your desk. I want to savagely tear your clothes off. Why won't you have dinner with me?"

Sophie walked to her purse and pulled out a travel tooth-
brush and paste. When Jake gave her a questioning eyebrow she
explained, "Old habit from traveling so much. And you need to
spend time with your parents."

"Why can't you come with me?"

"Oh, Jake. We're not ready for that."

He crossed his arms defensively. "We? Or you?"

"Neither. I don't want to wake up one morning and realize we
moved too fast and have regrets."

"What kind of regrets?" His defenses built a little due to the
hurt her words inflicted. But nonetheless, he willed himself to
listen.

"The kind that comes when you jump in headfirst before
knowing how deep the water is. Now, be a good boy and pick up
my papers."

She unlocked the door and left for the bathroom. Jake slid
into the office chair with the realization that she might have been
right. Dinner with his parents kind of meant relationship status.
What they had just shared was wonderful, out of this world, but
was he ready for more? Jake's body tightened in response, his
heart began to beat hard and fast. Nothing seemed more real
than that moment. He felt it, saw it, understood what was happening around him and to him. No, this was no panic attack—it
was the beginning of hope. An optimism that evaded him but no
longer hid in the shadows of doubt and fear.

* * *

Holy Crap! That is the naughtiest thing I've ever done. Sophie
could still taste Jake on her palette, and it was wonderful. She
never had a man want her the way Jake did. He was a potent

drug she desperately wanted to be addicted to. She craved him with a need that kept her up at night fantasizing, and this tiny fix wasn't going to be enough. She wasn't sure she would ever get enough when they finally stopped dancing around the inevitable. Brushing her teeth became a feat with all the smiling she was doing.

"Jake Sanders, you will be mine. We will make this work."

Reapplying lipstick, Sophie came to a sudden halt. Jake wouldn't be a one-night stand. She'd have to be prepared to deal with his demons—something she didn't know anything about but was prepared to learn, because that was what you did when you cared about someone.

Walking back to her office, Sophie heard him laugh at something Dave had said. She stopped and studied his profile. Jake looked relaxed, and he wore a smile that actually reached his eyes. Had she done that for him? The magnitude to which their lives might change if they started a serious relationship hit like a sniper bullet to its mark. Fast, precise, and deadly—to her heart. She was in love with him.

Sophie walked into her office and sat down in the very chair in which Jake had conceded defeat. His body was gone, but the memory of what happened still lay in the air with a sweet smell.

"I want this," she announced. "More than anything." Hearing his laugh again made Sophie's heart fill with joy and cemented her determination to learn more about his disorder.

Jake poked his head into her doorway. "Hey. I'm headed out to do some stuff. See you tomorrow?"

"Nope." She smiled when his face dropped in disappointment. "I'm just kidding, Jake."

"Figures." He came around her desk and pulled Sophie into his arms. She let her feelings soar as his lips pressed against hers.

Their tongues did a slow, unrushed ballet as the tempo of their hearts beat faster.

"Jake. Out."

"You have such a way with words." He began to kiss her again, but Sophie pushed him to arm's length.

"We had our fun today. Now, get the hell out of my office before I call in reinforcements."

"Lieutenant." He saluted her with a lopsided grin and left.

Sophie sighed. *Oh, that man gets cuter with every passing minute.*

Chapter 12

"Too bad she wouldn't join us," George pouted.

"No kidding. Our last night here and she flat-out refused. For Christ's sake, we were here for fourteen days!"

"Maybe you scared her off." Jake smiled at his parents. "You're both kinda ugly." The truth was, she had said she had some things to take care of. An appointment she couldn't miss. But in the back of his mind, Jake wondered if it had more to do with not wanting to take a chance on them being more than what they were—a casual relationship.

Renee shook her head. "She's been good for you. Look! Your sense of humor is back and there's a light in your eyes."

"I have to agree with your mother, son."

"Why does it have to do with her? Why can't it simply be because I'm happy? Or that I like what I'm doing?" Jake rolled his eyes when his father sat forward. He only did that when he really wanted to prove his point.

"Jake, I've always been proud of you..." his father began.

When Dave chuckled beside him, Jake sent him a warning glare.

"...never have you given us trouble. Well, except for the time with the blond girl in tenth grade. That worried us."

"What's your point, Dad?"

"You're a jackass," Renee announced to the whole restaurant. People turned to stare, but she didn't stop there. "You have something wonderful, right in front of you, and you're throwing it away by not taking the risk of being in a real, committed relationship. The least you can do is let your brother have a shot at her."

"What?" Dave asked.

"You heard your mother."

Dave cleared his throat. "She's really not my type, Mom. She's kinda bossy."

"She's not bossy, Dave." Jake turned and shot his parents a defiant look that mirrored the ones he'd given them as a teenager. "And you two only like her because of who she is."

George pointed an aggressive finger at Jake. "Don't talk to your mother like that. Yes, we respect her as a dancer. She's a very talented ballerina, but that has nothing to do with it. Waitress! Bring me another beer so I don't sock my son!"

Both Dave and Jake hid their faces in their hands. Their parents were never known for tact.

"What we're saying is you obviously really like her or you wouldn't have locked yourselves in the office together a couple of weeks ago. Oh, dear!" Renee turned to her husband. "Do you think that's why she wouldn't come out with us tonight? She's embarrassed about having sex with our son?"

"We haven't had sex. And, could you please keep your voices down. I told her where we were going tonight, and she said she might join us."

Jake's thoughts wandered to the outfit she had worn earlier. The slit on the knee-length skirt didn't look too daring until she

sat down at her desk. Then it opened to reveal the thigh highs
and garter belt she wore beneath. And the red high heels! He
almost swallowed his tongue when he saw them. Yet, every time
they were together and the opportunity arose for them to have
sex, he backed off. It seemed his mind and body were in a constant fight. He spent many nights pondering why she stuck with
him when she obviously didn't know where they stood as a pair.
Heck, he was confusing himself.

"Well," George announced, "We've already ordered the appetizers and drinks, so I don't think she's—"

And there she was, in pink cashmere with black slacks and
heals. Whatever his father began saying evaporated with the
sight of her. Unconsciously, Jake stood, and she smiled when she
saw him. His night became brighter, his life happier. And it all
had to do with the woman walking toward him with the doll-
like eyes and the understanding of a saint. It was then that he
knew—the world revolved around Sophie Agnés.

* * *

*What the hell was I thinking? What a total mistake coming here
is.* And yet, she threw caution to the wind when it came to trying
to stop her and Jake's bond from getting any deeper. She needed
to see him, hear his laugh, and simply be in his presence. With
frantic worry she tried on every outfit she owned, and then settled for the silky pink sweater she knew Jake liked. He'd commented on it one day and then couldn't stop touching her for the
rest of it.

"Hi." She knew she sounded breathless, but he stood there so
stunning in a suit jacket and tie.

He kissed her lightly and whispered, "You're beautiful."

"Don't manhandle the girl." George stood and pushed Jake away. "Give me a hug. We're so glad you made it. Actually, we were just talking about you."

Dave rolled his eyes. "Dear God, Dad. Don't embarrass Jake. I'll be hearing about it forever."

"I was only going to say how this is our last night here and we'd hoped she'd show up."

Sophie looked to Jake, who gave her a pitied look. "I'm sorry, I was held up. There were some things I needed to take care of."

Renee sat forward when Sophie sat down. "Like what?"

"Mom," Jake and Dave warned at the same time.

"It's okay, guys. I had some documents to sign." When Renee opened her mouth, Sophie decided she might as well continue. "I'm selling some property."

"Really?" George inquired, "Where?"

Sophie felt the faint blush come to her cheeks. "France, and here at Nantucket Sound."

"No kidding," Dave said. "Why would you want to sell the one in France?"

Sophie smiled when Jake gave his brother a light punch for asking the question. "I haven't been there in years. What's the sense in keeping it when you don't see it? Mostly I rent the space out, but I had a tenant that wanted to buy the property. I'm happy to get rid of it."

She ordered a beer when the waitress came to take her order. Renee was currently sipping on one, and Sophie always preferred it over wine. Even at her mother's disapproval of it not being a woman's drink.

The night stretched on and the more she talked to Jake's parents, the more she liked them. There was no artificialness about them. They said what was on their minds and didn't care if you liked it or not. She found it comforting not to have to walk on eggshells as she did with her parents and their crowd of friends.

When the meal came, Jake repeatedly asked his father not to talk with a mouth full of food. By the fourth time she couldn't hold in her laughter anymore.

"You both remind me of my uncle Rick—or Richard, as my mother likes to call him—and my aunt Estelle. They always made the party fun. I remember as a kid wanting to hang around them. My mother would shoo me away, but I'd always sneak back. To this day she says they influenced me beyond repair."

"Really? I don't think there's anything wrong with you. Except, of course, you like my youngest," Renee joked.

Jake's infectious laugh traveled through the restaurant. He swung an arm behind Sophie and pulled her to him in a warm-hearted hug. He seemed so relaxed, even in a restaurant with tons of people. She couldn't help her heart swelling with happiness. He always seemed a little uptight and defensive. But not tonight. This evening he was a man who secretly held her hand under the table and winked at her whenever she squeezed it.

When the bill came all hands went for it.

"The company will pick this one up," Dave announced.

"*I'm* treating you, since you complain I never pick up the bill."

"Jake," Renee broadcasted, "it's not that you don't pick up the bill, it's that we want to see you more often when we're here. You almost never come out with us."

"I've seen you every day for the last two weeks," Jake protested.

"He's a good son, Renee. Even if he hasn't swept the beauty beside him off her feet," George stated.

"Who says he hasn't?" Sophie chuckled, and with deft fingers, slipped the bill out from all their hands. "Since I have the bill and have not been able to attend these fun-beyond-belief outings, I'm paying." She had just opened her purse when George put his hand over hers.

"I prepaid." Sophie felt her mouth gape open as Dave, Jake, and Renee started to argue. "I hope next time you're not a stranger." George then leaned forward and kissed her cheek, but not before whispering, "You're good for my son. Thank you."

Sophie cleared her throat so as not to start crying. No one had ever made it this clear that she was welcomed into their family. Love bloomed for the couple before her. How could it not? They were wonderfully themselves, and they obviously cared very deeply for their children. She wished she could have the kind of relationship with her own parents that Dave and Jake had with theirs. Her heart broke a little for how things could have been different. There would have been more childhood laughter, sleepovers with friends, fun activities, and meals with parents she could talk to. And right now, she wouldn't be missing what she might have had if her mother weren't so controlling and cold.

"Dad? Are you hitting on my woman?"

Sophie blushed at Jake's declaration.

"No need to worry, son. Your mother is the only woman I've ever wanted." He then leaned over and gave Renee a scandalous kiss.

Sophie covered her mouth to stop from giggling. "My parents would die if they saw that."

Renee smiled. "Then your parents need to live a little."

The night had cooled to a bitter chill when they stepped out into the parking lot. They all hugged good-bye, and Sophie wished Renee and George a safe flight back. As Jake walked her to her car, Sophie wanted to ask him to stay the night with her; it was on the tip of her tongue. But when he kissed her brains loose, and Sophie melted in his arms, the only coherent thought that existed was how strong and thoughtful Jake was. How he liked to laugh and tease, but he still let the people he cared for know he wanted to be a part of their lives.

Admiring his family was easy, and she couldn't remember having a better time out with people who liked each other so much. Bruce's parents were as stuffy as hers. Never joking about serious things or raising their voices to get a point across. The rest of Sophie's old social circle was just as boring and in need of learning how "to live a little," as Renee put it.

Sophie was still smiling about dinner when she slid her key in and opened the door to her home. The building had once been an old factory and was now converted to condos. She loved the tall ceilings, the large rooms, and the fact it was all hers. In the doorway there were stairs to go up to her living space, while downstairs her dance studio called to her. She flicked on the lights to look at the open space. At the sight of her ballet shoes Sophie felt compelled to lace them on and begin to dance just for the fun of it. Not because she needed to stretch to keep in form, but for happiness and love. Jake was who she'd been looking for all her life. She'd sensed it from the moment they'd met. Well…when he woke up long enough to talk. Sophie laughed at the memory. Sure he had problems, but who didn't? They could work on everything together—she'd prove that to him.

Sophie's hand reached down to her pointed toe, a graceful ending to her impromptu dance. She followed it up with a squeal of glee.

* * *

Dave looked at his brother with disgust. "Why am I dropping you off at your house and not Sophie's again?"

"Because I'm not going to invite myself over."

"Truth time." Dave walked up to Jake's door with him. "And I want a beer."

"Scrooge."

"Yup. How was it?"

Jake opened the fridge and handed his brother a beer, "How was what?"

"You said I'd be the first to know. Remember?"

Jake downed half his drink and hoped to get drunk enough to not call a cab and knock on Sophie's door. "I haven't slept with her."

"Nope. But you had other fun."

"Dave, you need a woman."

"That's a given. Well?"

"Mind-blowing. After two years, I can't believe what I've been missing. Mom and Dad being around have made it next to impossible to get my hands on her. I feel like a teenage boy with out-of-control hormones." Jake finished his bottle and grabbed another.

"I still don't see why you don't just go over there."

"Dude, I don't know. I'm so unsure about all this. If I do that, it brings this thing between us to … to … shit, I'm not sure I want a commitment."

"Yeah. You wouldn't want to ruin the good thing you have going here." Dave swept a hand motioning to the empty walls in Jake's kitchen. "Bachelorhood's been great to you."

"Dave."

"Yup."

"If you're going to insult me, you can't drink my beer."

"Okay. Then I'm going to go. Have a few more drinks, and when they don't work with keeping your mind off of her, get your ass over there." Dave slapped his brother on the back and left.

Shit! Dave was right. Sophie's was where he wanted to be. He took his third beer out and started chugging. By the time he finished his fourth, he couldn't remember why he wasn't at her house.

* * *

She wasn't sleeping anyway so why bother lying in bed? Her head was aching, so she decided a couple aspirins and the book she never seemed to finish would help push her off to dream land. Sophie looked over at the clock next to her bed. Two a.m. and all was quiet. Maybe that was what was bothering her: the silence.

Her feet padded softly on the plush carpet in her hallway. She tied her silk robe at the waist as she headed for the kitchen. There was ice cream in the freezer. Chocolate. A spoonful would help fill the void of her empty home.

Sophie had never truly been lonely before, yet tonight, with the moon sending its silver beams through the numerous windows of her loft, she felt just that—and a longing to be understood. Right now her ex-fiancé was at the hospital having his first child. Of course, Bruce had called her as he was on his way there. He thought she'd want to know. And, why would she? They were through, and she was grateful about it. So what if his bimbo was about to give birth? Sophie actually felt no jealously or anger toward the woman, only pity. Because while Bruce might be faithful right now—and that was very hard to believe—he wouldn't be much longer. Eventually he would get bored of the baby and its mother. There would be too much responsibility for him to want to stay, and then mother and child would be alone.

She took the heaping spoon of ice cream with her to the large picture window, which faced the street in front of her home. The street was quiet, except for the taxi dropping some guy off. She nibbled on the dessert, appreciating every spoonful, when the stranger below turned into the streetlight.

"You have got to be kidding me." In a rush, Sophie tossed her spoon on the counter and raced down the flight of stairs to the street. The buzzer rang just as she hit the last step. Joy swelled inside of her. Anticipation made her fumble with the locks. She opened the door and found the only person on this earth she wanted to see standing there. "Jake, what are you doing here?"

"I needed to see you." He stroked her cheek with his thumb and gave her a little smile, "Can I come in?"

Sophie leaned against the doorjamb and crossed her arms. "What makes you think I want to let you in?" she joked. Even in the dim of her hall light, Sophie could see the flush creep up his neck.

"Oh...I don't know. If you want me to go, I will." He bit his lower lip and Sophie felt hers twitch.

"You're far too cute. A powerhouse of a man with a marshmallow heart. I can't believe you'd give up so easily. I was only kidding."

Jake stepped forward when she fisted the material of his shirt and started to pull him in. For the first time ever, Sophie felt anticipation's powerful grip. Her breath hitched, her body pulsed and the primal need to be with him, to love him, to share secret moments with him, washed over her. The ache in her heart made her head feel faint and her mind feel giddy. For this wasn't the beginning of a teenage crush but the sensation of two opposed worlds pulled together with such force that the inevitable collision would be catastrophic to anyone in denial. She couldn't calm her nerves from prickling in exhilaration.

"Oh, I wasn't going to give up that easily," Jake told her. His stare transfixed Sophie as he stepped into the front entryway then kicked the door shut behind him.

"You've been drinking." Her voice shook, not from fear, but from her racing heart and sexually charged body.

"Not as much as you think." He pinned her against the wall, grasped her ass and hiked her up so she'd wrap her legs around his waist. "Four beers to be exact, and only to convince myself not to come here."

"I want you, too, Jake. Please." At her pleading, he grasped the silk rope and nightie underneath, then tore. She cried out as Jake's mouth and teeth assaulted her breasts.

"Good God, you're built."

"I'm all yours." Fisting her hair in his hands, he brought his mouth to hers. Their bodies heated the small entryway. Jake made a move for the stairs.

"Up, right?"

"Yeah. Down the hall, bedroom on the left." She pulled his shirt over his head then began to journey over his chest with her mouth. When she came to one of his nipples, Sophie bit. His body reacted by tensing under her lips.

"Fuck it, honey. We're not going to make it."

He laid her on the stairs not far up from the ground floor. His mouth scorched her, his hands possessed her, and his greed seemed unquenchable. He tore the rest of her nightclothes open. Then in one swift move, pulled her panties off. She felt the searing kisses start at her ankle and hastily move their way up.

"I just want to devour you, Sophie. You're the most beautiful woman I've ever seen." His hands moved to her legs then opened them so he could taste her. His tongue and fingers worked her body to a fury, and she gripped the stairs to keep from bucking off.

"You taste incredible."

His hot breath tickled her small thatch of hair. She wanted to tell him how wonderful he made her feel, that she needed as much as he wanted. His tongue shot inside of her; his thumb rubbed her swollen numb. She erupted. And before Sophie recovered, Jake pushed inside of her.

"Oh, Jake!" He was huge. Filling and stretching her so deeply to accommodate himself. The thought that no other man reached her core in such a way before brought tears rolling from her eyes. She shifted her hips and brought her legs up higher around him. Jake grunted and pulled them over his shoulders then started to pump hard. With his lips on hers, he placed one hand under her bottom to bring her body up to meet him. His other arm supported his weight on the stairs as Sophie held on for the ride of her life.

Panting and unable to make coherent thoughts, she heard her lover say, "Put your legs down around my waist." She did as she was told and soon felt her body rise—they ascended the stairs as one. He held her tight to him, never slipping out and every few moments plunging deep again. With her lips on his shoulders and neck, Sophie gave as well as she took. Her hands snaked around to grasp his ass.

Jake seated her on something cold and hard—her kitchen table. When he laid her back over it, his teeth seized one of her nipples. Sophie cried out then moved her hips faster. The feel of him overwhelmed her. She didn't know where to put her hands or how to move. All she knew was that he felt magnificent.

He stood before her, tall, muscular, and devilishly handsome. His possessive hands traveled down her until they found where their bodies were joined. He touched her with light fingers, bringing her urgency to a new level.

"Go over for me, Sophie. I want to see what I can do to you. How I can have you come for me with the slightest touch." He didn't move inside her but only used his hands on her body to touch her soul. When she couldn't take any more, her body bowed without permission, and she felt her peak begin. At the end of what she was sure to be delicious delirium, Jake slowly pulled out the whole, wide, long length of himself, then pushed it inside her hard. Sophie heard herself cry out in triumph. On top of her again, he pumped fiercely. Her nails gouged into his back, but she couldn't stop herself. The ecstasy he brought her went on forever, and when she thought she might go mad from it Jake kissed her hard. When he convulsed inside of her, Sophie's body tightened one more orgasmic time, causing Jake to let out a howl and her to release one last, spectacular time.

* * *

Jake tried to shift off Sophie's trembling body.

"Please don't move yet," she told him.

"I don't want to crush you."

"Then I'll die a happy woman."

Her eyes were closed and a small smile played on her lips. He kissed her before resting his head on her shoulder. "I don't know what to say."

" 'Wow' comes to mind."

He chuckled and squeezed one of her breasts. "I only came to snuggle on the couch with you."

"At two in the morning?" Sophie snorted.

He felt the beginning of wanting her again, felt himself starting to stir. "You know, two years of abstinence has taught me a lot of self control." He smiled when she looked at him blandly.

"Really? You could have fooled me. By the way, where are we?"

He looked around her kitchen, "Not really sure. We might have busted through the wall and we're now on your neighbor's kitchen table."

"They're jerks, anyway."

"They might be thinking that about us, after all the noise." He twitched inside of her. "Wanting you is going to be a problem, Ms. Agnés."

She brought her lips to his, but before they met he saw something in her eyes. Was that love? He tried to dismiss it, but his mind stumbled over the thought.

"What's wrong?" she asked.

With her hands on his face, Jake found himself speechless. Instead, he showed her what his mind couldn't wrap itself around. He did his best to be gentle when he picked her up into his arms and kissed her longingly to prove he was capable of being tender. The he carried her in his arms down the hall to the bedroom, where he laid them both down and showed her what he once promised: slow lovemaking. She was all that mattered and all he needed to survive. Sophie opened her heart to him. He felt it. Yet in the depths of his mind, he wasn't sure if he could accept it.

"I need you," he told her.

"Love me," she whispered.

Her request crumbled every guarded wall he'd built over the years. She adorned him with soft kisses and slow movements filled with affection and longing. When Sophie rose above him, Jake grasped her hips.

"No," she whispered and brought his hands to her breasts. "I'm yours to touch, taste, and love. I'm yours." With her lips to his, she sealed the promise, then wrapped them both in euphoric bliss.

He'd never experienced anything like it. Their bodies seemed to move in unison—knowing what the other needed before asking. Her kisses sent shivers of emotions straight to his heart where they swelled and left him astounded.

Jake rolled Sophie onto her back. He then kissed her shoulder and slowly moved up to her jaw. "I can't explain what I feel for you." Did he say it aloud or to himself? It didn't seem to matter, because Sophie's arms brought him close as they moved together slowly. He couldn't get enough of her taste, her feel. Nothing ever felt so right, and for the first time in years he opened up to someone without caution—a gift she gave to him without knowing it. Their eyes met, and Jake struggled for the words he couldn't find to explain the hurt, need, and passion she evoked in him.

"Only you," Sophie whispered.

Jake nodded in agreement while their bodies showed them what their minds had yet to fully comprehend.

Love.

Chapter 13

It was after eight in the morning when he woke. The bed was empty, but her scent still permeated the air. They'd made love one more time before sleep and exhaustion took them over. Jake smiled at the ceiling. Damn, he'd forgotten how awesome sex could be. And with a very limber woman, it was unbelievable.

He jumped out of Sophie's bed and grabbed a throw quilt to wrap around himself. Her bedroom walls were deep red, and her cherrywood bed had detailed ivy posts that reached to the ceiling. The wrought-iron crown held a sheer white canopy, artfully laid so as not to overwhelm the eye. It was apparent that Sophie liked the finer things in life. The bed itself must have been worth thousands, and that wasn't counting the matching dressers and end tables. Jake shook his head in wonder. She sure was a classy lady.

Turning from the extraordinary bedroom, which was almost half the size of his house, he told himself not to be overwhelmed by the house's huge rooms, wide hallway, and tall ceilings. The photographs that adorned the walls were black-and-whites. Some were of Sophie with friends, others scenic countrysides, and others...Jake tipped his head at the picture of a dog peeing on a tree.

He decided he liked it, along with the close-up photo of a cow's nose.

By the time he made his way down the corridor, it became apparent Sophie worked because she wanted to, not because she needed to. The living room was done in a soothing burnt orange. He found himself wanting to relax on the rich chocolate leather couches that sat before a massive stone fireplace with a pellet stove built into it. Sophie was efficient and, even with all her money, was still conscious of cost.

In the kitchen Jake found his clothes neatly folded on yellow granite countertops, along with his backpack. He dropped the quilt and quickly dressed. The soft green kitchen comforted, but the fresh coffee called to him. Finding a mug, he drank down the dark black liquid with gusto. But even without the caffeine boost, Jake felt ready for anything. And after he found Sophie, he hoped she was, too.

The music floated up the stairs, the soft romantic sonata beckoned him to find its origins. When he came to the bottom of the landing, natural bright light illuminated the dance hall and had Jake thinking of guardian angels and the heavens. Vast mirrors lined the walls. A wooden barre stretched the length of the room, and long, sheer vanilla curtains graced the massive windows. But it was the woman at the center of the room that stole his attention. She moved with flowing grace. Her eyes were mostly closed, and her lips wore the whisper of a smile.

Jake sank to the wooden floor and watched. She mesmerized him. Every move she made, effortless. The music changed tempo and her body moved with it. Sophie leaped through the air and landed with natural ease. Then she spun around while circling the room. He couldn't take his eyes off of her. She became the center of his world, if not only for that moment, then for what he started hoping would be forever. The trance she placed on him was an enchanting prophecy of what could be. His heart welcomed it, and his contrary mind couldn't break the spell. He saw his future laid out on the floor she now bowed low to. The promise of a ring, the grandness of the day, and forever to live their lives as one. When she looked into his eyes, Jake saw children. Without a word, he rose and left the room. This was too much, too fast. When he heard her behind him, Jake turned and enfolded her in his arms.

"Promise me you'll be understanding and patient." He pulled back and gazed into her enormous blue eyes. "I want this so bad, but I need something."

"What, Jake?"

"I don't know. There's a missing part of me that I can't move on without."

"Don't give up on us. We can find it together." When a tear slid down her cheek Jake thought he would come undone. The last thing he wanted was to cause her pain.

"Maybe. Tell me this is enough for now. That—" He lost his words when the doorbell rang.

"Jake, I promise." She kissed his lips. "Go jump in the shower. I have a feeling that's my father. He joins me for morning coffee a couple times a week."

Jake couldn't help the grim look that crossed his face. "They'll never approve of me."

She slapped his ass and shooed him along. "If they did, I wouldn't care for you."

Damn, if he didn't almost tell her that he'd fallen in love with her. What the hell was he going to do? *Play it out. See what happens.* His therapist had always said to take it one day at a time. Boy, he hated doing that.

Jake quickly undressed, turned on the water, and stepped under the spray. The double shower head made him smirk. Sophie obviously liked pampering herself. He wondered what he could do to please her. Maybe an afternoon picnic in the living room? That was how his buddy Mitch reeled in his wife. Or a bubble bath with champagne and chocolate. The thought of her in a warm tub with him made Jake hard.

When the bathroom door opened, he called out, "What's up?"

"Nothing."

Then he heard a giggle.

"You sure?" Arms wrapped around him from behind and he couldn't help but smile when one of her long fingered hands took hold of his proud manhood.

"What have you been thinking about?" she asked.

"You, me, and a warm bubble bath." Jake turned and poked her in the belly with it. "Think you can wash me up?"

"Oh, yeah." Sophie grabbed the soap and started lathering up his chest.

"I thought that was your father?"

"Nope. Mailman." After washing him up completely, she handed the soap to Jake and purred, "Your turn."

"My pleasure." Jake took his time, all the while rubbing his body against hers, then they rinsed off under the soaking spray. "Turn around and place your hands on the wall. God, you have the most wonderful ass." She moaned when he trailed a finger on her shoulder blade. "Now that's a surprise." The butterfly on her shoulder blade beckoned him to trace it with his lips.

"My own little rebellion."

"Oh, I think you've fought back in more ways than this." He bent her over and began to tease by slipping three fingers in and out of her velvet lining. "You're so wet."

"Damn, Jake. Don't taunt me."

He slipped his fingers out and traced them up between her butt cheeks to the cleft of her ass. "Spread your legs a little more and roll up on the balls of your feet." He positioned himself behind her, taking his time to taste her skin and squeeze her breasts.

"Jake," she said on a breathless plea.

"I want to hear the pleasure I'm giving you. Don't hold back." He penetrated her welcoming warmth, all the while keeping a tight rein on his control. Carefully, he moved a little more into her, his breath and body straining for release. "You're so unbelievably tight in this position." When Sophie moved her hips in a circular motion, Jake let out a winded breath.

"More!" she demanded, and he gave. Inch by excruciating inch, Jake went deeper. Sophie braced her hands on the shower walls while he gripped her hips. With his sudden plunge, she cried out and, given her position, he buried himself deeper than ever before. The abrupt passion that seared through his body left Jake motionless and panting. He tried to back out, just a little, but her inner walls gripped him. Breathless from the squeeze and the pleasure Sophie brought him, he snapped.

Frantic for her, Jake couldn't get enough, feel enough. She cried out in ecstasy and met his every powerful thrust. When he felt her body show agitation with the position, he spun her around and pinned her to the wall. With his mouth capturing hers, Jake took them on a sexual journey of lust-filled delight.

He'd had sex with many women, even made love to a few of them, but he'd never felt this connected to one before. Every pleasure he felt, Jake knew she felt, too. Her whimpers and moans, the way her body responded to his. He came once and never stopped. Just kept going—control gone. They were now on the bathroom floor. His hands needed to touch her everywhere. His mouth sought to taste every inch of her slickened skin. When she arched under him, Jake became blinded by the need for release, but Sophie sought other ideas and left Jake no option but to trust her.

She twisted, pushed, and finally got him to roll. When she rose above him, Sophie moved as a bull rider would for his eight-second thrill ride. Holding on, Jake yelled for mercy. He needed to fight for control, he desperately grasped for it—but in the end, he was incapable of having it. Sophie took it from him, and the only thing Jake could do was believe she wouldn't abuse it.

Always the one in charge, Jake was accustomed to calling the shots. People looked to him for decisions and commands, and they trusted him with their lives. "Power comes with a price," Jake was once told. This was why he always dictated with careful consideration. And why what happened that night, when his men died and his best friend bled out in his arms, was Jake's entire responsibility.

"Jake," Sophie whispered in his ear. "Let go. I'm here for you."

Opening his eyes, tears streamed down his face as he erupted inside of her then bellowed in pain. He gasped for air as Sophie pulled him into her arms and held tight. Years of self-loathing, torturous dreams, and sleepless nights all came to the surface. He cleansed his soul and then some. Weeping for his fallen comrades, weeping for himself.

She stayed as he babbled on about what happened—gory details and all. She soothed and whispered what in his heart he knew to be true, but his mind kept questioning.

"Jake, it wasn't your fault."

It was midnight—

The stillness, deafening. Gunnery Sergeant Sanders strained his ears to listen, but the only sound he heard was silence. The strategy—avoid the enemy and survive.

Jake's job was to keep it clean, not kill as many of the enemy as he could. In his mind the scene before him appeared to be the same as the many that had come before it. Another poor country ravaged by war. More dead civilians, casualties of a government mad with power.

His eyes tried to pierce the night and see though the blackness to what lay ahead for his men. No animal sounds or wind. The calm put him on edge with a premonition of doom while his feet moved quietly along the forest floor.

A small sound perked Jake's mind to attention. With his weapon tight to his chest he put a fist up to signal his men to freeze. Then he placed a hand to his ear indicating for them to listen. Nothing. Something wasn't right. Jake's skin crawled with an almost painful realization—it was too quiet, and their targets were absent from their posts. The reality gave him the impression that turning back was their only real choice. But the military didn't like decisions based on gut feelings and fear. They wanted concrete answers and proof, and Jake had none.

He motioned his team to continue to the flank position over the rocky terrain. They were Marines, members of a brotherhood made for action with the defined values of Courage, Honor, Commitment. His team consisted of six well-trained men to infiltrate this enemy compound. It looked eerily abandoned through his nightscope. He wiped sweat from his eyes. There was no way they were too late. Their intelligence wasn't wrong and neither was he. Jake's lines of attack were always executed without consequence. But his gut told him this time would be different, even though everything had been planned out, down to the breakfast they would eat upon return.

With a quick gnaw on his lip, Jake split his teams up. The voice of James Callahan, his next in command and friend, came through to his ear.

"Gunny, I don't see a fuckin' thing."

"Stay cool." Jake slowly advanced. He concentrated on his breathing while adrenaline pushed him. Patience was a must to the win. Wait 'til they showed themselves, wait 'til you had a clean shot, wait for—

Something hot and quick whizzed by his face. "Down!"

But it was too late. Plunging fire came from the trees, the ground, and the air. The only way he could identify their place of origin was to look for the flashes of light illuminating the muzzles of the enemy's weapons.

Confusion and fear tried to grip Jake's mind. His throat tightened, and he quickly responded via radio to the other teams. Jake forgot about easy Sunday morning drives, video games he liked to play, drinking with his buddies, and his fiancée at home, along with the other life he lived there. None of that mattered. All that was important was getting his teams to safety.

"All teams target upper northeast fire." He belly-crawled to the man lying behind him. Without turning him over, Jake knew the man was dead by the mangled flesh of his throat. Helpless, Jake crept on to those still alive from the ambush.

"Gunnery Sergeant Jacob Sanders calling for immediate extraction!" A shot ripped through the upper flesh of his arm. He swore crudely and started calling out orders. His men were fighting with gusto and bravery, but Jake knew with the amount of arsenal the enemy possessed, they were outnumbered.

He signaled for two men to grab their fallen comrade as he knelt and laid cover for them. Through the chaos he heard an explosion to his right. The bright illumination created a midnight sunrise—

a beautiful deception that rained earth down upon Jake, then blinded him for what seemed like an eternity. With blurry vision, he dropped his body flat to the ground. His ears rang and his mind screamed, Move! *Jake stumbled and dashed to the shelter of a tree then pulled his M16 tight to his chest.*

The only explanation was somehow the enemy had known his team was coming. His plan had been perfect; they always were.

Shouting more orders, Jake moved to a kneeling position and started taking the enemy out, one by one. No wasted shots, no panicked fire. He calmed his mind and concentrated on saving his men. The skirmish before him moved in slow motion as reality disconnected from his mind. He heard not the screams, only the programmed commands for this type of situation shooting automatically from his mind to his mouth. The whirring sounds of the evac chopper might have brought a sense of hope if Jake hadn't seen men dragging the fallen or wounded to it.

A painful crack sliced through his consciousness, numbing out the anarchy and blood. He stood there, his eyes seeing the world before him through a window; torrential rain poured down its panes, warping the view of the outside. The body holding him up shook, neither from fear nor anger. It quaked from the distance his psyche created from the truth he was living.

"Gunny!" Jake heard the calling from a distance he couldn't quite pinpoint. The limbs that hung from his shoulders twitched as his mind escaped the fractured reality and came back to the immediate.

"Callahan, where are you?"

"We're southeast from your point and screwed with sustained fire!"

Jake redirected himself, as a watery bog filled his mind and kept his thoughts slow. He passed two wounded, one being dragged by the other to the pickup point. His body halted to a stop so he could stare at them in confused disbelief. Where did his brain go? What was happening?

"Damn it, Sanders! Where are you?"

That's right! He was supposed to be helping Callahan. In a full sprint, Jake leaped over a fallen tree then up a rocky mound before catching sight of his comrade. He began to fire at random with erratic short bursts. When a high-pitched squeal infiltrated the air, he fell flat to the ground as more dirt rained on him. Or was it? Stunned, Jake twisted his body and knocked off the heavy object that landed on his back. It rolled to the ground palm up. The ring on its wedding finger winked at him in the dim light of arsenal fire.

"Jesus," he heard one of his men shout.

Jake bellied over to the man and, once again, tried to blink the confusion from his mind. "Let's move." The words came from his lips before he fully comprehended the scene.

"I think I'm hit."

Jake's brain switched back on while he looked down at the tattered remains of the man's leg, nonexistent below the knee. "You'll be fine, Private. Stay alert."

"Yes, sir." The man sounded strained from running on shock and adrenaline. He pulled his M16 to combat position to cover Jake.

With a nod Jake bellied away from the injured man as the firing around them stopped. Not a good sign, and that truth weighed heavy on Jake. Either the enemy fell back on guerilla tactics, or now they were combing for hostages. He spotted a small group searching the ground and bushes. Flanking his adversary, Jake took the shots and killed three. The fourth man fired while retreating and hit Jake in the side. He fell to the ground in breathless agony then rolled on his back to bring a bloody hand up for wound inspection.

"Shit."

Reeling from the pain, Jake couldn't comprehend the man over him speaking. He just nodded while the fog in his brain became thicker, disassociating him from his surroundings. His head buzzed and his body became heavy as he tried to help the man who half-carried him toward safety.

"Wait!" Jake shouted, distracted with disbelief by something he saw in the freshly blasted ditch. He fell to his knees and dragged Callahan up and out of the hole until his torso lay on Jake's lap.

"Callahan."

"Gunny, we need to go!" Looking up, Jake saw men fighting a battle that shouldn't have happened.

"We need to get you out of here!" the man repeated. But, Jake's mind left his body as he looked down and into the lifeless eyes that stared back at him. With shaking hands, he slapped Callahan.

"Up, soldier! We need to go!"

The rapid firing started again. But Jake could only stare at Callahan's blood-spattered face. His chest showed no wounds, his dog tags glinted in the arsenal firelight, and there was nothing left below his waist.

The impatient private pulled at Jake. "I will drag you if I have to," he told him.

Jake's eyes moved over Callahan's legless trunk. Confusion pulled at his awareness while he, once again, looked through that watery windowpane to the world outside. "I don't understand," he said more to himself than the men trying to help him. Jake spread his fingers so the blood gushing out of the torso, lying across his lap, could flow through them. "Where's the rest of you?"

"We're going now!" The private pulled him away as the men surrounding them fired, suppressing the enemy for their escape. Jake looked back one more time to see his friend being rescued . . . and then there was nothing.

Chapter 14

The pounding headache saved Jake from the most awful dream. He'd been at Sophie's exploring her wonderfully erotic body, then things went horribly wrong—he had a flashback and ruined everything. Jake rolled over and buried his head in the pillow. She had been sweet and understanding, but—

"Hey, I know you can hear me."

Jake felt the poke at his side and let out a growl.

"You know I don't scare easily." She pushed a little more, and with a sudden realization, Jake sat up to attention.

"How the hell did I get here?" When Sophie looked at him puzzled, he realized it hadn't been a dream after all, and he was in her bed naked.

"Jake," she said patiently, "I want you to take these aspirins."

He looked at them with a heavy sigh. "It wasn't a dream."

"No. But I wouldn't have wanted it to be. You have a hell of a stamina."

Instead of taking the pills, Jake leaned forward and kissed her lips. "I'm so sorry."

"For what? Being you? Shit, Jake. There are some men who haven't gone through half of what you've seen and done, and they're in the nut house. You're stronger than you're giving yourself credit for. Now, get off the pity potty and take the damn aspirins." She gave him a weak smile and then a kiss.

"What time is it?" When she didn't answer and nodded to the white pills, he gave up and swallowed them.

"It's four in the afternoon."

"What?"

"It's four—"

"I heard you. I just can't believe it."

"You needed the sleep. I'll make you a sandwich. I washed your clothes from yesterday, so why don't you take a shower and meet me out in the kitchen?"

"Will you join me?"

She laughed and kissed his lips hard. "You're lucky today is Sunday and our day off. Now don't push your luck. I'm having a hard enough time sitting down today from all the frisky activity."

"You're just trying to make me feel better about—"

Sophie reached up and pushed the hair out of his eyes. "I don't have to make you feel anything because you know it's okay. Otherwise, I'd have kicked your firm ass out. Now you smell and need a shower."

Jake watched her walk out without a glance back. How lucky was he? He found a woman who seemed to understand and accept who he was. A dark shadow draped his thoughts and dragged him down to the hell in which he was accustomed to living. Why would he voluntarily subject a person he came to deeply care about to the horrors in his life? *Step back now so no one gets hurt.*

* * *

Sophie's jaw ached from being tight with worry. After Jake had purged himself, body and soul, he'd been spent. She practically carried him to the bed then cleaned him up. After that, he slept peacefully in a slumber so deep that at one point Sophie put her ear to his chest to make sure he still lived.

"Breathe," she told herself aloud while leaning on the kitchen counter for support. He's fine. Watching him have a flashback scared the living hell out of her. She reflected about the day he'd called into work and she'd gone over to check on him. Jake warned her this was how he lived, never knowing when one of these episodes was going to occur. Now she'd fallen head over heels for him, and the thought of Jake going through this alone was torture. He needed her, even if he wasn't going to admit it.

When she heard the shower turn on, Sophie busied herself with making him a sandwich and preparing herself mentally. She knew he was going to try and end it—she saw it in his eyes. Well, she'd just have to cut him off beforehand.

The phone rang and the caller ID announced Dave calling. She'd phoned him not so much in a panic, but with concern wanting to know how long Jake would sleep, if he would wake up with a headache…whether or not he was going to therapy to make himself better, or if he was on a downward spiral of doom.

She picked up the receiver. "Hello?"

"How's it going?"

"He's just getting in the shower. He seems okay, Dave. But I won't know for sure until he comes out of the bathroom."

"Make sure you do some stomping around. You don't want to come up behind him."

She let out a long breath. "Dave?"

"Yeah?"

"Is he getting help for this? I mean, is he talking to anyone on a professional level?" Sophie began to chew on her thumbnail. This was a question she had wanted to ask Jake, but under the circumstances she didn't want to upset him further.

"Yes. I'm not sure how much else I can say without him wanting to beat me up." Dave's laugh sounded strained. "He's not a big fan of people knowing."

"I can understand that. How about you? Is there something for the families to help support people with..." She paused in hopes the right words would come.

"Yeah, there is. I go to a group once a month that's open to anyone. You can come with me, if you want."

"I'd really like to do that, thank you. Umm, Dave?"

"Yeah?"

"What did he do for the Marines?" Sophie moved from biting on one thumbnail to the other.

"A lot, Sophie. And then some." The silence on the phone became tangible as both their thoughts went to the man in the other room. "He's come a long way. When he first got back and came out of the hospital, you couldn't get him to leave the house. He'd been hit pretty bad. First with the bullets, then by that bitch of a girlfriend he'd had. She didn't deserve him, and I hope she rots in hell."

Sophie chuckled. "Why Dave, I've never heard you speak so highly of anyone before."

He laughed, "Yeah, well she comes in every now and then. Don't worry, though, you'll get the privilege of meetin' her sometime."

"Oh, goody. Can I hang all over Jake when she stops by?"

"You can toss him on the bar and have your way with him…
as long as I'm not around. Although I would love to see her face."
Another pause, and then, "She called the other day to see how
Jake was doing. Wanted to know if he ever talks about her."

"I don't need to get my claws out, do I?"

"They're always out, aren't they?"

"Ha ha!"

"Keep your eyes open. I never liked her, but I like you. And
you make my brother happy. He needs you, Sophie."

"No pressure, right, Dave?"

"Nope. Just don't mess with him and be straight or I'll make
you suffer."

"That's why I like you and your family. You're up front. I'm in
love with him, Dave, but I can't tell him. I think he knows, but
he has to deal with his feelings first."

"And here I was hoping you two were just havin' fun for the
hell of it."

She heard Jake heading down the hall. "Listen, he's on his way
to the kitchen. I have to go."

"Thank you, Sophie."

"For what?"

"Caring enough to stick around."

"He's going to need a crowbar to get rid of me."

Still a little shaken from the night before, Sophie started
banging around the kitchen to make sure Jake knew where she
was. She then switched the music to a station he liked.

"You make a lot of noise."

"Yeah, well we know I'm not the most graceful of creatures
when I'm off the dance floor." She smiled, hoping he'd return it.
When he hesitated, she kissed him and handed over the plate of
food. "Sit and eat."

"Aren't you having any?"

"I had breakfast and lunch. You, my dear, skipped both and had a hardy workout." She sat across the table from him and began caressing her hand over the smooth finish. With her desires inflamed, Sophie's imagination recreated the erotic activities from the night before.

"What are you smiling about?"

"Oh...I was just thinking about all the use my table has gotten lately."

He grinned playfully at her. "It's the perfect height."

"So tell me Jake, are you going to eat and run home, or are you going to take me to the movies?"

"You want to go to the movies? Don't you think we should talk about what happened?"

Here it comes, she thought. "No. Not unless you want to."

"No, I really don't, but feel I owe you an explanation."

She searched his eyes and found the hurt he felt he'd inflicted on her. "Jake, you had a breakthrough—"

"I don't know if I'd call it a 'breakthrough,'" Jake said with air quotes. He pushed his plate away then got up to pace the kitchen. Agitated, he pulled at his hair and she heard him ground his teeth.

"Well, I know I'm new at this and everything, but have you ever let go like that before?"

"You know what, Sophie? I don't think I want to talk about it." In reaction to his sharp tone, her defenses rose. She pressed her lips together and checked her temper before it showed. Jake needed understanding and someone to vent to, not a harsh argument.

"Jake, if you don't want to, then we don't have to." Folding her hands on the table, she waited for him to reply. When he only stared at her she asked, "What?"

"You're crazy! I fell apart in there! What kind of man does that? I've attacked you—"

"Don't even go there," she said, slapping her hands on the table and jumping to her feet.

"I hurt you," he yelled.

"Your brother told me not to go to your house and I didn't listen. What happened is *my* responsibility, and you can't have it!"

"What? You're nuts."

"So what?" she said in a calmer voice. "I'm nuts about you."

"How could you be? I'm a wreck! Most the time I'm wondering who I'm going to hurt or let down next. I couldn't keep my team safe, for shit's sake—how the hell am I going to protect you?"

"Why do you think you don't deserve to be happy?" His shoulders slumped, but she pushed anyway, hoping he'd come to terms with some of what happened. "It wasn't your fault. War isn't fair, Jake. You all knew the risks when you joined. So did the troops you were with."

Jake turned his back to her. "My best friend had his body torn in half. I never remembered that until this morning. At least before, I couldn't picture it in my mind. Now...it's there."

Her heart ached for the military man he was and the wounded soldier he'd become. She took a chance and went to him, hoping he would let her hold him. Leaning her head on his back, she began stroking his arms. "I want to help. It's an honor to have you trust me enough to let me in. That's what you did, Jake. And it's going to make you better, stronger."

"I just want things to be the way they used to be. It was perfect...I was—"

"Jake, perfection is an illusion—a lie. True perfection is learning your boundaries and being able to live inside of them."

Jake scoffed, "Can you do that?"

"I'm learning to. It's not that bad." She turned him around and pushed a stray hair out of his face. "You need a haircut."

"I started going back to group counseling. I think I'm ready to join the world again."

She pecked him on the lips while joy of his admission swelled her heart. "I'm so glad. We've been waiting for you."

"I believe I could trust you with my life, Sophie. But can you accept that's what I used to take from other people?"

She answered "Yes" without hesitation, and he pulled her into his arms.

Chapter 15

I'm Jake, and today I'm going to work on finding me." He looked around the room and saw Doc Murphy staring up at the ceiling, as usual. He wondered what he could say to make the guy's day a little better, but couldn't come up with anything that didn't sound like bullshit. He had to take it one day at a time. Everyone there understood what he was going through. It all seemed so belittling, because really, how could one person understand another person's demons? When it came to the military, they all did something different, and they were all dealing with it the best they could. Jake finally settled on saying nothing at all.

"I'm Murphy. Today I'm going to work on getting everyone off my back." He met Jake's stare.

"Good luck with that," Jake told him. Everyone laughed a little. Even Doc grinned.

The next hour passed with tears, shouts, and questions. Some people could relate to each other, and some couldn't. The lost and somber feelings Jake experienced in prior weeks slowly gave way to hope and the realization he had learned to live in the moment. The elation gave way to a smile on his lips.

"Jake, how are you feeling today?" He pulled himself out of his rambling thoughts and focused on the team leader, Charlotte.

"I'm good."

"Really? You haven't said too much today." She looked at him with a mixture of concern and pity. Jake really hated that expression.

"I'm good. Just wondering where I go from here."

"Where do you want to go?"

"If I knew, I probably wouldn't be asking." His answer was short, a little bitter and he regretted it as soon as it came out. "Sorry."

"Very frustrating, isn't it? Most of us ask that question even though we haven't been through what all of you have. Jake, where do you want to be in a month?"

He gave a little laugh. "I don't know. I've been thinking about shopping."

"Do you go out to shop?"

Doc gave Jake a good-natured hit on the chest. "Out to shop? Hell, my groceries are delivered!" There were murmured agreements and a few chuckles.

"You should try Big Y on Tuesday mornings, Doc," Jake informed. "Hardly anyone there."

"Maybe next week."

"Really?" Charlotte said to Doc.

"Oh God. Now she's going to try and set us up, Sanders. I'm sorry, two men in the grocery store looks gay. Now, I don't have a problem with that lifestyle, but I'd really like to be picking up the ladies, not giving them mixed signals."

"All good on my end," Jake announced.

"That's right. You've been dating a woman. How has that been going, Jake?"

Jake turned and looked at the leader. "Okay."

"Just okay?"

"I'm thinking of getting a cat."

"Really? Why?"

"Well, I have trust issues, and I'm thinking if I start with something small, eventually I'll work myself out of this funk."

"Sounds reasonable. What's your girlfriend think?" At Jake's silence the room looked to him for an answer. "Have you talked to her about the trust issues? What are the reasons you have them?"

"Why do any of us have them?"

"But, what are *your* reasons?"

Jake shifted in his chair. How did this conversation move to him? Hadn't he diverted the attention away from himself fairly well over the past few weeks? "I just don't think I can trust myself, so how can others trust me?"

"That's a good question. Anyone care to answer it?" Her eyes scanned the group. "No? Jake, who are you?"

His eyes darted around the room then rested on Doc, who only shrugged his shoulders. "I'm Gunnery Sergeant Jacob Sanders of the Marine Corps."

"Yes, but *who* are *you*?"

Shaking his head, he told her, "I don't understand."

"Before we can give a part of ourselves, we need to know what part to give and trust that it'll be taken care of. Now, I'm not saying that starting a relationship is wrong. But if you're questioning yourself, make sure you're spending more time concentrating on you, and not the relationship." Charlotte looked to the group to include them. "This is the time to be selfish. You need to work on you, before becoming part of a 'we.' Some of you have spouses and feel the pressure to make it all okay. It's not going to happen overnight. And it's certainly not going to happen if you distract yourself from getting better. Jake?"

He gave a low groan when she picked him out again. The last place he wanted to be was the center of attention.

"What are you going to do for yourself today?"

He looked around him as his mind moved in a million different directions. "You know, I haven't been missing any time lately. I've been able to control my temper and go grocery shopping on other mornings besides Tuesdays. The woman I've been seeing is funny, smart, and beautiful. Yet I feel it's unfair because I'm always holding a part of myself back from her."

"What part, Jake?'

Jake shrugged, "That's the problem—I'm not sure. I don't know myself enough, and maybe that's why I don't trust every thought I have." The realization left a suffocating weight on his shoulders. He had suspected he wasn't ready to play house yet. But there'd been something about Sophie that made him want to know who she was. What made her smile, laugh, cry? At night, did she read herself to sleep, or did she simply drift when the urge came to her? How many times did she take bubble baths in her fancy tub? Did she burn everything she cooked, or was she exaggerating about it? But finding those things out wasn't why he was there. Group was about rediscovering things about yourself. Your own favorite color. What made you smile, laugh, and cry.

"Sophie and I really just started this datin' thing. I care for her." Jake fell silent for a moment. "Is it too much to ask her to wait?"

"Wait for what, Jake?"

"Me to be ready."

Doc grunted, "If you find a woman that will wait for you to

stop being crazy, hold on to her. Lord knows my wife wasn't up for the job."

The counselor looked at each of her patients. "None of you are crazy. And asking the person you care about to understand that you need more time is not asking too much. You must think about *your* needs and make the right choices for you. Don't worry about what other people are thinking or how they're reacting to your actions. You're responsible for your decisions and thoughts. No one else's."

"I was responsible for other people once, and they died. I can't go back to that. I don't want the pressure of having someone count on me again." Jake looked down at his hands. When another hand covered his, he was shocked to see it was Doc offering him comfort. Jake nodded to show his appreciation—it seemed the only thing Doc could do without getting too close to someone. However, the gesture helped Jake feel understood and supported. A breakthrough for the lost doctor who almost took his own life.

"Learning who you are will come with time. Jake, what are you going to do for yourself today?"

An hour later, Jake walked to his truck while small white flakes fell from the sky. The snow covered everything with its angelic grace and cleaned the dirt from the dingy world around him. Sadness overpowered the hope he'd felt earlier. What was his favorite way to fall asleep? How did he like his steak cooked? Sophie went to make him one, once, and he freaked at not knowing.

She always talked about kids. How cute one was that she saw while shopping. How her cousin's kid began to walk. There wasn't any doubt in Jake's mind about it; Sophie would want them. But did he? Could he handle the responsibilities that went with them?

Starting his truck, Jake stared out the front windshield. Life moved on with or without him, and he was sick of missing out. He wanted to be a part of the world that brought happiness and joy to one's heart. He needed it in the worst way, and now he knew how to get it…by taking care of himself. Such a simple answer, and yet, it was something he needed to force himself to do.

A hawk soared down to land on a tree branch in front of him. The bird looked directly into Jake's eyes and let out a screech, as if to say, *Well? What are you waiting for?*

"Nothing," Jake said to the empty truck cab. The windshield wipers swished back and forth, pushing at the fallen snow obstructing his view. Then Jake's new friend fell forward into a gentle glide and swooped away. Jake wanted to be that free. To know where he was going and have confidence in himself.

"Today I'm going to really start learning who I am. That's what I'm going to do for myself."

More determined than ever, Jake put his truck into reverse. He wanted Sophie in his life, but right now he needed to find his way into an existence he could live in freely. Hope that she'd stick around bloomed, while dread leaked black doubt into his heart. This decision threatened to pull him down into the doom of depression. But instead of giving into it, Jake surprised himself and found anticipation. He only wished Sophie would show the same compassion she'd shown him from the first moment they met, because breaking her heart would be necessary to obtain his goal.

* * *

"Dear, I really think you should come."

"Mom, I don't want to." Sophie paced her office with the cordless phone to her ear. Sometimes her mother was more than pigheaded; sometimes she was an absolute pit bull.

"You need to stop these self destructive ways you've taken up. Your father and I are not here to pick up the pieces of your life."

"I didn't ask you to."

"No, you didn't. But that's what a parent does."

"A parent wants what is good for their child. Something the two of you seem to have forgotten when it comes to Bruce."

"This isn't about Bruce. You've made up your mind when it comes to him, and as we all know, there is no changing it once that happens."

"What do you want from me, Mom?"

"I want my little girl to be happy."

Sophie tapped her foot on the chipping tile floor of her office. "So, you both have realized what a slime bag Bruce is?"

"Why must you use language like that?" Sophie heard her mother give a small huff. "We want to spend a night with our daughter. Is that too much to ask?"

Her mother sounded overly sincere, Sophie knew there must have been something Antoinette wasn't telling her. She could feel the trap being laid, and she knew she had to be careful. "Can Jake come?" At her mother's hesitation, Sophie knew her assumption was right.

"Sweetie, he can come another time. We really wanted it to be us."

There it was: the slight high pitch in her mother's voice when she wasn't quite lying or telling the truth. "Who's 'us'?"

"Now don't get upset, but your father and I have a friend, and his son is in town."

Sophie gave on impatient gasp. "You've got to be kidding me!"

"He's only in town for the holidays, and—"

"I'm not going." Rage filled Sophie, but she tried to stay reasonable.

"Sophie, please think about this. We already told him you were coming along. We can't go back on our word."

Sophie growled, "Then you shouldn't have given it."

Antoinette became quiet for a moment. "It would mean a great deal to your father and I. You know how your father has been down since he lost all that money on the stock market."

"And this is a way for him to make new connections to help make up for the loss?" Sophie's voice became too quiet, even for her own comfort—a surefire sign that her temper was about to reach an epic high. While it did bother her that during the crash her father lost money on numerous investments, her parents hadn't lost everything. Very little, in fact, when one looked at her parents' entire estate.

"We need to come together as a family, Sophie. Your father and I have always been there for you."

Sophie's temper boiled as she tried to remember if her parents had ever supported her instead of pushing her into doing their bidding. The sad fact was she couldn't. With her voice under restricted control, Sophie began: "I can't be a part of this. I'm sorry. I won't be roped into your world again. I'm not on this earth to help secure bonds with your friends, political or otherwise. You and Dad are just going to have to find another way."

"After everything we've done for you!"

"Mom," Sophie's patience waned but she refused to be pushed into a shouting match. "As a parent it's your job to do just that. Not make me your puppet for affluent gain."

"You are coming, and there is no way around it. Be ready this Saturday at four p.m. The limo will be picking you up. I want you to wear the deep blue dress with the low cut in the back, and for goodness' sake, go to the stylist. I won't stand for that dreadful blond. Do you hear me, young lady?"

"Mom, I'm not going, and that's final!" Sophie hit the End button on her cell. She would have given just about anything to see the look on her mother's face when the call disconnected in her ear. The woman was insufferable. She didn't know when the line was crossed, and Sophie wondered if she even cared.

Sophie wanted to punch something, anything. Her day was not going as well as she had predicted. The morning started off sunny and warm, for late autumn weather. Then by the time she needed to go to work, it had clouded up, gotten bitter cold, and started to snow as if the end of the world was coming. Her back windshield wiper broke, leaving her view hindered and danger-ous. Then she skidded into her work parking space and almost hit Dave's truck.

Sophie pulled her hands through her now red hair. The color change seemed like a good idea. She'd been a brunette all of her life, and she'd decided to try every color until she found something she loved. Dave had commented that it matched her personality. What the hell was that supposed to mean? She wrapped herself tighter in her woolen winter coat. Something had happened to the heat in her office, leaving it so cold Sophie swore she could see her breath. The stupid repairman was delayed due to the weather, because apparently, a lot of people were feeling the sudden freeze.

Wiggling her toes to make sure they didn't get frostbitten, Sophie looked at her computer harder than she needed to. Some-how today the numbers weren't working out right with last year's figures, which was going to be a problem with Thanksgiving, Christmas, and New Year's just around the corner. "Why the hell did they put all the holidays at the end of the year?"

"Because it makes everyone miserable," Dave answered her.

"And that's exactly how I feel. What's up, Dave?" She rubbed her hands together and blew on them for warmth.

"Why don't you move some stuff out front so I don't find you frozen into a Popsicle? Come on, I'll help."

"I should just go home. I'm feeling a little useless today."

"Why?" He sat on the edge of her desk. "You're anythin' but."

"Nothing seems to be going right. I don't know what happened this afternoon to have everything going crazy. Plus, I just hung up on my mother." She looked at him with sorrowful eyes.

"Not a cool thing to do, Sophie."

"I know. But she kept trying to get me to go to dinner with them and some friend who has a son. I mean, really? What's wrong with her?" After slamming a fist on the desk, she rose and started gathering some papers. "You going to help me move this crap? Or sit there and watch?"

He laughed, "Oh, I'll help you. But if you keep that attitude with me, I'm dumpin' you in the fourteen inches of snow we're getting."

"Fourteen!"

"You should watch the weather more often. The day just went from stormy to blizzard." He grabbed a stack of papers and left her staring at him.

"Dave! Please tell me you're joking!" Sophie yelled out, charging from her office. She jolted to a stop at the sight of a familiar-looking, short brunette with blond streaks talking to him. She was the mystery woman from the Halloween party. From the displeased look on Dave's face, she also concluded it was Jake's ex.

Without thought of consequence, Sophie walked up to them. After placing her armload of files down on a table, she turned to Dave, who stood uncomfortably between the two women. "Who's your friend, Dave?"

"Ummm..."

"I'm Shawna." The woman extended a hand. Sophie looked at it with a raised eyebrow.

"Really? You want me to shake that? You're Jake's ex, aren't you?" The description Dave had given her was dead-on—a trashy-looking brunette with no fashion sense and too many piercings. And, right now, she looked very confused. Well, Sophie should clear that up.

"Yes, but I don't see what that has—"

"No, you wouldn't," Sophie interrupted. "Are you here looking for Jake?"

"Not your business," Shawna scoffed.

"Listen, girls," Dave began, "I don't think this is the time—"

"Oh, but Dave, I do. The place is empty and now I understand why my day has been going so badly. It's been preparing me for this." Sophie took a step toward Shawna, whose eyes grew large. Their faces were mere inches away from each other when Sophie began. "What the hell do you think you're doing? You don't belong here and no one wants you here. You're white-trash stench is stinking up the place."

Shawna's mouth fell open. "What? Who the fuck do you think you are? Dave, who is this person?"

Dave held up his hands and stepped back.

Sophie smirked at him. "You're a smart man." She turned her attention back to Shawna. "Get out of our restaurant," she said between gridded teeth.

Shawna crossed her arms. "No. I don't know what your problem is, but I've done nothing to deserve this. Dave, will you please get rid of this person?"

Sophie heard him laugh and it made her smile. "I'm Jake's girlfriend and I don't appreciate you sniffing around. He doesn't want you, and if you don't get your ass out of here, I'll remove you myself."

"I'd like to see you try."

Sophie pounced as a starved animal would on helpless prey. She grabbed Shawna's hair and yanked her toward the door. Shawna bellowed out in pain, and then swung. Sophie caught the fist in the jaw and let go. Next thing she knew, they were both on the floor rolling around. Fists and knees hit hard-bodied surfaces. Sophie could taste blood from her split lip, but she gave one good blow to Shawna's gut, then stood over her.

"Get out!" Sophie hauled Shawna to her feet then threw her out the door where she landed at Jake's feet.

"What the...?" Jake looked down at his ex and then at Sophie, who stood with her confident chin in the air.

"I told her she wasn't welcomed here and she refused to leave."

"Jake! She attacked me!"

Jake looked down at Shawna then stepped over her to Sophie. "Your lip is bleeding." He dabbed at it with his jacket sleeve.

"Hello? I could sue your asses for this."

With a snarl, Jake turned, "Shawna, you know you're not welcome here. What the hell do you want now?"

"I love you, Jake," Shawna announced with pleading eyes while bent on her knees. "She's not the woman for you. I was blind. Please take me back. I'm so ashamed. You're the best thing that ever happened to me—"

"Your lies won't work, Shawna. You weren't there when I was shot, when my friend died. You only made everything worse. Why the hell do you think I'd take you back or listen to your blundering, self-serving excuses and apologies, now?"

"Because I love you. I never stopped loving you." Tears streamed down her face, and Sophie scoffed at her. "Look at her, Jake! She's evil. I didn't do anything to start this fight. She came up and just started swinging. I didn't deserve this! Please give me another chance."

Jake put his arm around Sophie and started to steer her back into the building. "You walked in, that's what you did. Go back to your lover, Shawna. I have nothing for you. No feelings at all. Not even disgust. That's how much I don't care."

"You'll get bored. And then you'll come running back to me!"

"I doubt that," Sophie told her. "I'm not a cold fish." She stuck her tongue out and laughed when Dave stopped Shawna from attacking her. A very humiliated Shawna backed up and ran to her car.

"Jesus, Sophie," Jake took her behind the bar and grabbed a dishrag to clean up the blood on her face and hands. "What the hell were you thinking?"

Without fully understanding why, a tear spilled down her cheek. "She hurt you so bad, Jake. I just wanted to pound her face in."

"Well, I'd say you did a good job. We'll be lucky if you don't get arrested for battery."

"You're mad at me." She looked down at their joined hands.

"Actually, I'm a little turned on. But that's the perverse side of my mind. The other side is yelling at you and not understanding what you were thinking."

"I wasn't thinking."

"No shit."

Her lips twitched when she looked up and saw him smiling at her. "I was going to kick her ass down the street but you kinda interrupted that."

"And I was going to let her," Dave said. "I told Shawna, again, not to come back. She said she was gonna call the cops. I reminded her that I repeatedly told her she's banned from this establishment and she took it upon herself to come here and suffer the consequences. If she wants to call the cops, go for it.

But she'll be on the losing end." Dave sat on a stool and looked around the empty bar. "I think we should close up due to the weather. Jake, why don't you drive Sophie home, or something? She's had a shitty day."

"I just got here."

"Don't whine, Jake. You weren't the one scared out of your mind when Shawna walked in. I knew Sophie was gonna kill her and I'd have to help bury the body. Happily, of course."

Looking thoroughly amused, Jake told his brother, "As long as I don't have to help. I've wasted enough time on her." He gave Sophie a gentle kiss, "Go get your jacket, slugger. We're going to my house. It's closer."

Chapter 16

With his eyes closed Jake gave a winded breath. He wasn't happy. "I still can't believe you did that," he said.

"Me either. I swear I've never been a violent person. It's only recently." She leaned over and began to kiss his naked chest. "I like this." Her hand snaked under the sheet to tease him.

"Sophie. You've tired me out. I need fuel." He climbed out of bed quickly and pulled his jeans back on. Before leaving the room he turned and looked at the woman stretched naked across his bed. Her striking red hair fanned out over his pillow. Unable to resist her, Jake crossed the room and laid his body over hers, "You look so content."

"Hmm. I am." Lazily she stroked a hand through his hair while Jake studied her. "What are you thinking about, Jake? You have that crease between your eyebrows."

"I'm looking at your bruised face." He really hadn't been looking at the black and blues coming to the surface under her eye. No, his heart had been trying to revise his future plans, their future plans, by searching her soul for any unsavory feelings toward his condition. Seeing if the unwavering confidence she showed in him was waning. Trust—he really needed to learn how to do that again. But it was so damn hard, and he couldn't quite explain why the fight upset him.

"Don't remind me. Can you imagine what my mother is going to say? Aaaggg!"

"Why did you attack her?"

Sophie's eyes looked sharply into his. "Because she deserved it. I'm not letting you go without a fight, Jake. Get used to it."

He felt his mind take a painful step back. "Excuse me?"

"You heard me," she teased with a nip at his earlobe.

He tried to pull away to a safer position but found himself trapped by her legs. "Let go, Sophie."

"I don't think so. What's the problem, Sanders?"

She was joking around and he was serious. Why couldn't she see that he truly had a problem with what happened? "I want to know why you tried to smash her face in."

"I just told you," she snickered and grabbed his butt.

"No, you gave me a line of bullshit." To no avail he tried, once again, to get off of her.

"First of all," she said with a determination that matched his mood, "you're not going anywhere. Second, that wasn't a line of bull. I was justified in doing that to her."

"I could peel you off me if I really wanted to. Now, let me up." The challenge came out before he thought it through. Knowing Sophie was knowing that she backed down from nothing.

She lifted her chin. "Try it."

He grabbed her legs and tried to strip her off. When he'd almost succeeded, she wrapped around him like a boa constrictor—the more he fought, the more he lost ground.

"What the hell! Sophie, get the hell off of me!" Jake tried to stifle the chuckle that rose in him.

"No."

He managed to slide her around him so they were face to face. "What the hell is your problem?"

"It wasn't a line of bullshit, Jake." She puffed out her bottom lip in a pout.

"Yes, it was. I saw it in your eyes. Why did you attack her? Did she say something to you?" Sophie released her legs from around him, leaving Jake to think he'd won this little war. He smiled at the thought, but then he saw her somber face. "She said something."

"No, she didn't."

He watched her choppy movements while she dressed and wondered what her problem was. Why wouldn't she just tell him? He didn't need to be protected from Shawna. He was over her and in lo—he stopped himself before his mind could completely form the word. He couldn't be in love with her, could he?

"Jake, I promise you, she didn't say anything. I just care about you so much that seeing her threw me into a rage. I'm sorry."

Oh God, he was in love with her. He had to stop this before it went any further, before he caused her any more harm. Jake closed his eyes so he couldn't see the hurt he was about to inflict upon her. "I can't do this, Sophie."

"Yes, you can. You just don't know it yet. I'm going to get some ice cream. Want some?"

"This is way too much pressure." His words stopped Sophie at the bedroom door.

"That's not true," she whispered.

"Yes, it is. When I look at you I see children and picket fences. A dog running around in the backyard. Sophie, that's not for me. My moods are unpredictable. In the end, it was a good thing what happened with Shawna—us breaking up, I mean. I know that now. Can you imagine what it's like not knowing if you're going to seriously hurt someone you love at any moment?"

"You're scared," she whispered with disbelief edging every word. "Are you still in love with her? 'Cause if that's what this is about, I want to know!"

For the first time in their relationship, Jake felt like he possessed complete control over what was about to happen next. With that power his heart sank to his stomach and he did what he realized he should have done a long time ago. "No, I'm not."

"Bull. You wouldn't have this much of a problem with me punching her face in if you weren't." Her chest visibly heaved and Jake struggled to get her calmed down.

"I haven't felt anythin' for Shawna in a very long time." Jack put his hands up in the air to try and halt her anger.

"Then why are you using *her* to break us up?"

"I don't want to get married, Sophie. I don't want kids and dogs. I like that my house is quiet and I have my alone time." He watched as her head bobbed up and down as if agreeing with him.

She then walked to him and when they were toe to toe, Sophie accused, "You're a terrible liar."

"It's what we need. I'm not a part of your fancy world."

She pushed a finger so hard into his chest Jake thought she would drill it through him. "That's not my world and don't you dare use my upbringing as an excuse for you wimping out on us."

"Sophie, I'm a mess."

"Okay, so first it's that you don't want what you think I want. Then it's my whole childhood and money that's getting between us. Now, it's that you're a mess. Which is it? Because I'm getting really confused and it's been a long day."

"All of it," he said, standing his ground. She needed to know a life with him wasn't going to happen right now because he needed to focus on getting better. Building a relationship would only be a distraction. It was just as the counselor said: he had to figure out what he wanted and needed before he could give himself to someone else. He wasn't sure why he couldn't just tell her that; but Sophie, unwittingly, had given him the out he'd been looking for when she fought with Shawna. Now he was going to use it to his advantage. "I'm breaking this off." He saw her body jolt back and Jake instantly swore at himself for hurting her.

"So, let me get this straight. I punched your ex and you got all hot and bothered about it. But now that we've had our roll in bed, you want to breakup?"

"Yes…No. Yes, I want to break up. No, it's not because we had sex."

"Really?" She stepped back from him and tilted her head to the side. "If you look at this from my view, that's exactly what it is."

He watched her walk to his dresser and pick up a forgotten glass. "Sophie…" he warned, but was too late. It crashed against the wall behind him and he lunged at her to stop anything else from being thrown. She jumped out of his way and picked up one of his shoes and hit him in the head.

"Bastard!"

"Damn it, Sophie!" He dove for her again, only to land hard on the floor, facedown. Looking up he saw her scurry across the bed. Leaping in time to grasp one of her ankles Jake pulled her under him. He pinned her with his body and secured her arms above her head.

"Stop fighting me! It's what needs to be done. I don't want to but I have to."

Sophie gritted her teeth. "Let me go."

Panting, Jake looked down. Her eyes were fiery with defiance and she leaned to the side in an attempt to bite his arm. It was perverse, but Jake couldn't deny the hard-on she gave him. The passion and love she displayed even in anger tore his resolve to shreds. He became wild and took her without restraint. Jake couldn't control the beast that was suddenly, violently, let free. He plundered her body with his own, driving into her. When she screamed his name amidst the passion, he moved faster and harder. Punishing them both with the need they couldn't sate.

They rolled off the bed and hit the floor in a pile of limbs and unbridled fury. As their bodies slapped from the sweat that soaked them, the sweet scent of sex filled the air, creating a natural endorphin they couldn't deny. Anger welled within Jake. She tore down his walls, and while he should have been happy, the devastation was too painful for words. Something opened inside of him while he felt another part close. Not sure whether he was winning or losing the battle, Jake plunged them over the edge where no reason existed, only sensation.

* * *

Sophie's mind and body felt beaten while her heart broke for what they'd built together and would never have.

"We had angry sex," she said aloud, before she could stop herself.

Jake rolled off of her and covered his eyes with his forearm. "I'm so sorry."

"You say that an awful lot, Jake."

"And, I mean it... every time."

Uncomfortable with the silence that grew between them, Sophie got to her feet in an attempt to dress. She picked up her shredded panties and tattered bra. "Gee, Jake. Did you leave me anything to wear?"

He gave her a slow grin, "Sorry."

"No, you're not."

Jake kneeled on the bed and pulled her to him. When he rested his head on her chest, she let out a long breath. "You're right, I'm not. Sophie, I don't want to let you go, but I need to work some things out."

"So, after all of this, you're still breaking up with me." She walked away from him, unsure as to what to say.

"Sophie, please." Jake grabbed her hand before she could get too far. "Please...look at me."

When she did, all emotions filled her. Anger, for loving a man who wouldn't admit he loved her back. Sad, for knowing Jake might need more time than she was willing to give. But most of all, scared that when he was ready, it might be too late.

"Jake...this is bullshit. But I have no choice but to respect your decision."

"Sophie, it's for the best." He stood before her, visibly trembling.

"Really? For who? Because all I see is being miserable without you."

"You need time. You just broke up with Bruce a few months—"

"Hold it one minute." Sophie couldn't believe he could come up with more pathetic reasons. "You're going to use *him* now as an excuse?"

"Please hear me out."

"No, I've listened to enough of your reasons. You're a coward, Jake."

"Excuse me?"

"You heard me! You're a coward and I'm done with this conversation. Take me home." Choking back a sob, Sophie looked around for clothes to wear.

"Angel. We're just getting to know ourselves. How can this work?"

His voice was soft and patient, but it didn't do anything to calm her anger. "Don't call me that. What happened between yesterday and today? Or had you always been thinking of a way out?"

"I guess it's been simmering there for a little while. Sophie, it's not you, it's me."

She laughed openly at him. "Oh...my...God! You did *not* just say that, you ass! I was prepared to fight for you, to make sure you knew how much I loved you. I *do* love you, Jake!"

"Sophie, I need to learn to fight my own battles. It shouldn't have been you that kicked Shawna out."

"Coward," she murmured under her breath. It didn't escape her notice that he hadn't reacted to her proclamation of love.

"I'm not a coward," he hissed through his teeth. "The truth is, if I'd been forceful about it, Shawna wouldn't still be thinking there's a chance. I want to be able to toss a CD on the shelf and not be a nervous wreck because it's not in its place. How about going to the mall? I haven't been there in years. I want to go this holiday season. My house walls are bare—where are my happy memories? The pressure of this—" he waved a hand between them "—is a lot on me."

"A lot on *you*? I guess I don't count in this equation."

"Don't say that because you know it's not true. Deep down you know I'm right and we both need time, and maybe you should date other—"

"What! I want to go home."

They both looked out the window and saw the snow piling up

outside. *Great,* Sophie thought, *the perfect way to end the worst day of my life.*

"Ummm...why don't we wait—"

"Take me home or I'm calling a cab."

Jake went to his dresser as Sophie wiped a tear from her eye. Her world crashed down hard, and she just wanted to be home to wallow in self-pity. Not even her breakup with Bruce felt this devastating.

Jake handed her one of his sweatshirts. "I tore your shirt."

She snatched the offered apparel and avoided looking him in the eyes. He didn't deserve her understanding; his actions justified murder. And if he wasn't careful, she would deliver his sentence.

"Sure you don't want to stay for dinner and wait for the weather to let up some?" She narrowed her eyes at him with a look to kill. "Right, let me clear off the car."

* * *

The slow ride to her home was agonizing and silent. With every swish of the windshield wipers Jake contemplated what to say. He couldn't understand where he'd gone wrong. They went from laughing and making love to fighting and breaking up. Was that really what he wanted? Jake ran a hand through his hair in frustration. He hated feeling so confused.

"Sophie—"

"Don't."

She hadn't said anything since telling him to take her home. The tension between them was gut-wrenching.

"I really don't want things to end like this," he told her in an attempt to get her to talk. "We're going to be seeing each other at work and..." Sophie let out a long, agitated breath. "Okay, if you're not going to talk to me, I'm going to say what I need to say."

"Save it."

He glanced her way. She was stuffed in the corner of the passenger seat by the door—as far away from him as she could get. When she wiped at her eyes his teared up. "I'm sorry. I never wanted to hurt you. I'm just trying to find myself."

"You have an amazing way of saying the wrong thing, so why don't you just shut up?"

It would probably be the best thing, but Jake couldn't do it. He couldn't end things like this. He needed her to understand his reasoning. He wanted to come clean.

"No Sophie, I won't. I care a lot about you. I told you at the beginning that I didn't want to be in a relationship but—"

"Let me out." She opened the door, causing Jake to slam on his brakes. The car came to a sliding halt.

"Are you crazy? The car was moving!"

"Yeah, like five miles an hour because of this stupid storm. Good-bye, Jake."

She got out of the car before he could grab for her. "Damn it." Jake charged out of his vehicle. "Sophie, wait!" He went for her at a full run, and when he caught her she spun around and smacked him hard across the face.

"Jake Sanders, you're the most horrible person I have ever met, and I don't ever want to see you again."

"That's fine. But, I'm not letting you walk home, even if it's only a few more blocks. Get in the car!"

"No!"

Determined to do the right thing, Jake picked her up and threw her over his shoulder. Her fists beat him but he didn't mind, because he fully deserved it. "You're getting in the car so I can bring you home. I promise I won't say a word the rest of the way."

"Like your word counts for anything, anyway."

Her words cut him more than any bullet ever could. And the tears raining down her face almost floored him. What had he done? She was right. He was a coward and didn't deserve her.

The rest of the short drive seemed to take an eternity. He kept his promise and didn't say anything, though he really wanted to. When he pulled in front of her building, she got out then disappeared inside without a backward glance.

It served him right for breaking an angel's heart. Jake turned the car around and headed back on the treacherous roads. At the last minute he turned the wheel and headed for the Hungry Lion. He needed a drink. Just as he came upon it, he turned again. He didn't need a drink—he needed his big brother.

Chapter 17

Y ou're an idiot."

"I'm very aware of that, Dave."

"What did you tell her?"

Jake winced, "That it was me and not her."

"Ouch."

"Yeah, that's what it felt like, too...when she slapped me." Jake looked into his bottle of beer. "She called me a coward."

Dave snickered. "So what are you gonna do now? Stop workin', hide in your house, and wallow in self-pity?"

"This isn't funny. I'm seriously in trouble here. I don't know what the hell I was thinkin'. I mean, I do know, but I just didn't think it would hurt this bad."

"Really?" Dave finished chopping an onion then swiped them into the pot. "You stayin' for dinner or lookin' for another suicide mission of self-destruction?"

Jake glanced out the kitchen window where the whiteout conditions made it impossible to see. "I think I'm staying the night."

"Okay, but if I wake up in the middle of the night with you gropin' me, there's gonna be a problem."

"Ha ha. I'm sleeping on the couch."

"Yeah, and I've seen you sleepwalk."

Jake gave out an exhausted breath. His heart hurt and his stomach turned with disgust. Even his head hammered with a constant pounding for the idiot thing he just did. "You got any aspirin?"

"Bathroom cabinet."

Jake started sulking down the hallway when he heard his brother yell, "But it's not going to help with being a dumbass!"

"Thanks! I can always count on you for support!" Jake fired back.

Grabbing the aspirin and a cup of water Jake sat down on the toilet lid and held his head in his hands. There had been a time when Sophie had nursed his head with the same stuff. Too bad she wasn't there to help now. Course, she was the reason for all his pain, and no matter what anyone said, he did the right thing. They needed space and time along with...he couldn't think of anything else to make their breakup so imperative. *Shit, I'm so confused.* How was he already missing her? Weren't they supposed to go sledding or something this weekend? Jake pulled his cell phone out of his pocket. She'd been so upset. The hurt in her eyes tore a gaping wound in his chest. He wanted to know she was okay, but he'd only be playing with her heart if he called.

He dropped his head in shame as his phone hit the floor. There'd never be another woman like her. Every time Jake was with her he felt more alive. He only had to look at her to feel the world around him. The possibilities she gave to him were limitless. He wanted that feeling of hope she brought to him and the security of love and understanding. Jake's mind stuttered over that one word—*security*. *What about her* safety?

He could think of nothing else to do, so he returned the aspirin to its home. A jarred candle, waiting patiently to be lit on the sink counter, distracted Jake from his agony. Dave wasn't a candle kind of guy, so their mother must have left it during their parents' visit. Popping off the lid, Jake breathed the vanilla bean scent in. It tickled his nostrils while ambushing his mind with a memory of Sophie having a candle like this in her bathroom.

"I'm pathetic," he said aloud. He'd run from her scared out of his mind using every excuse he could possibly think of. The truth was, he couldn't protect her, and Sophie deserved a man who would and could fight for her. The trust she instilled in him was misplaced. He wasn't who she thought he was. Yes, that unwavering confidence in Jake helped show him he could still have faith in the world, but what good was it when you didn't have it in yourself?

Jake gave a rough sigh. Their relationship had ended before it ever really began. He'd never brought her to that movie or the theatre to make memories they could share. In spring they could have hiked the mountains of New York and witnessed the trees beginning to bloom. Camping in the woods, cooking over an open fire, her hair clad in a handkerchief; the image formed a smile on his lips before the reality of it never coming true melted the dream away. Where were those plans now? The pleasure of laughing together or being content in silent understanding— they were all gone.

Tears flowed down Jake's face. It hurt to feel. It also felt foreign. After years of being dissociated, he still didn't know what to do with all the emotions running through him. Hurt, anger, loathing for himself and happiness. *Happiness?* Yes, because he had felt those things and they were surprisingly good. The emotions mattered enough to him, she mattered enough to him, that Jake's mind registered the pain of loss. He guessed it could be considered a breakthrough, but he wasn't about to celebrate the bitter sweetness of losing Sophie and gaining sensations.

"Hey." The single soft word turned Jake to his brother. "Jake, it's gonna to be okay. Trust me." Dave put an assuring arm around his baby brother.

"It really feels like hell, man."

"Yeah, I would think so."

"Dave, I'm so pissed right now because she made me fall for her. And I'm pissed at myself for being such a wussy." He slammed both his fists on the bathroom counter, the candle rolled into the sink from the tremor.

"Don't break my bathroom, Jake. Go downstairs and work out until I have supper ready. You'll feel better."

"I don't wanna work out! I want to be with Sophie!" Jake screamed. With blind rage he pushed Dave away with both hands.

Dave caught his balance and yelled back, "Well, you can't! It's over for now, and you're just gonna have to deal with it!"

"I don't want to deal with it! I want things like they were before!"

"Before what?"

"Before I was all screwed up!" Jake screamed. "When I had my own mind. I wanna be normal, God damn it! Is that too much to ask? Because I'm thinking it is. To have a life and settle down with a woman I love without the baggage or fear that I might hurt her, physically and mentally. Sophie isn't prepared to deal with someone like me. She doesn't understand the life-and-death situations I've been in—"

"Neither do I." Dave ran a shaky hand through his hair. "Jake, I didn't know what to do in the beginning. But Ma, Dad, and I learned. Sophie will, too, because she loves you."

Jake stared at his brother so long he started to wonder if he'd ever have a thought to speak. She did say she loved him, but he had ignored her. He really was an ass. "How would you know?"

"That she loves you?" Dave scoffed at his brother. "You know it, I see. Hell, everyone sees it. Give yourself some time, Jake. You'll come around and know what you need and want."

"I want Sophie."

Dave started counting off on his fingers. "You want to be present, to settle down, and to have things like they were before. You want to be—"

"—normal," Jake grumbled.

"You want an awful lot."

Jake blustered, "So?"

"No one can have it all. Not even us, quote unquote, normal people. You need to get a grip."

Jake took an aggressive step toward his brother. Fury and hurt fueled his words, "Really? And what do you suppose I should do to get a grip? You seem to have it all worked out. Know what it is I need? Tell me big brother, Mr. Reformed Troublemaker, what do I need to do to fix this bullshit life I have? What can I do to be happy and not this miserable bastard I've become? I'd love to know. Please tell me. Or, do you want to call Mom and Dad first? You seem to always be gossiping about me with them. The three of you could have a powwow and come up with the next thing Jake should do."

"You're an asshole. Don't come over here feeling sorry for yourself and then expect me to take the abuse you're dishing out. I have a life too, Jake." Dave gave Jake's chest a little shove. "A new one I've put on hold for you. We all did, because that's what family does! Get off your friggin' pity potty and start standing on your own two feet. I've had enough of this. I back you up, I go to meetings, I do your shopping, give you an incredible amount of leeway at work. A business you half own but hardly put any work into! If you want all this shit, then you better learn how to stand on your own, because I won't be one of your crutches anymore."

Jake's chest heaved with fury, as did his brother's. Their breaths pulled in with short gasps and exhaled in low growls. It had been a long time since the two of them fought it out. Perhaps too long.

"Get out of my house, Jake. I don't care if you have to walk in that blizzard outside. But I don't want your unappreciative ass here."

Dave's voice was much too quiet. Jake recognized the warning signs signaling that his brother was ready to blow, and that could be a very bad thing. Dave wasn't quick-tempered but when pushed he was deadly. Jake had learned that lesson a time or two when they were kids.

Choosing his words carefully, Jake said, "If it's all the same to you... I'd like to go downstairs to work out."

Dave continued to glare at him.

"I'll stay out of your way for the rest of the night, and in the morning I'll be gone as soon as the sun is up."

Dave turned and walked out.

* * *

"I wish I never met him," Sophie sniffled into the phone. "God! Why do I have to work with him?"

"I don't know," Kathy told her on a long breath.

"This is so unfair. He's only thinking of himself, you know. He wanted his roll in the hay, which was way too awesome to ever forget. Damn it! Then just like that—" Sophie snapped her fingers "—he was gone. I'll never talk to him again." She blew her nose for the millionth time. Used tissues were spilling out of her bedroom wastebasket that she didn't have the strength to pick up. "He told me that he needed time to grow. That *we* needed time to grow. Can you believe that?"

"What a schmuck."

"I know! When he asked if I would stay for dinner, I thought about grabbing a kitchen knife and cutting out his heart so he'd understand what it felt like."

"We can only hope he's feeling like the slime bag he's being. Actually, I hope he feels worse than...than...I don't know. Just so bad he doesn't know what to feel or do."

"Like me?"

"No, honey. *Worse.*"

"I don't know how I'm going to face him at work tomorrow." What had she been thinking when she decided to seduce Jake Sanders? He obviously had a clear bright neon sign above his head that read: CAUTION. LOTS OF BAGGAGE. But, nooooo. Sophie wanted to make her own decision on what type of man she wanted to date and it burned her in the ass. If she had been thinking with her head and not her...she'd almost thought *heart* instead of *hormones.* Damn, she was a prisoner in Jake's war. Right from the moment she'd set eyes on him, her brain went MIA.

"You're right, Kathy. I'm going to go in there tomorrow and show him exactly what he's going to be missing out on. I made the first move at the beginning of this mess, now he's going to have to fix the disaster he turned it into."

"Atta girl! Wear the red heels, too." At Sophie's lack of response, Kathy asked, "What's the matter?"

"Those are Jake's favorite pair."

Kathy said, "Oh, you totally need to wear them. Where's your inner bitch, Sophie?"

"Defeated." She blew her nose again and swore at the soreness the tissues inflicted on the now-tender skin.

"No, she's just feeling a little down right now. Do what feels right."

"Nothing feels good." Another tear rolled down Sophie's cheek from her weeping heart.

"I know."

The next day the roads were cleared despite all of Sophie's prayers that they wouldn't be. She had hoped for a biblical-proportion storm, but instead she got one that dumped ten inches—not enough to close down New England. Everything was salted and sanded. She frowned out the window and drank her coffee, its black bitterness energizing her after a sleepless night. Her face was clearly a puffy mess while the look of forlorn sorrow hung in her eyes. She wouldn't beg. No, if he wanted her, he'd have to do the pleading. She wasn't going to talk to him, either. Misery was what she hoped to put him through.

As it turned out, Jake wasn't there when Sophie arrived at work. Only Dave, and he looked ticked.

"Dave?"

He grumbled at her.

"I have to do a lot of … umm … stuff today in my office. So you probably won't see me."

"Sure, Sophie," he said, never turning from the clipboard in front of him.

"Are you mad at me?" There was no way she would be able to handle it. If Dave was mad and not talking to her, she might as well give up and leave. Tears stung her eyes as the thought of her new friend hating her started to become overwhelming.

Dave turned. His eyes grew wide when he took in her appearance. She hadn't thought she looked that bad in the simple jeans and sweatshirt. Her hair was pulled back in a ponytail and her makeup had been applied very carefully to cover the dark circles. Apparently, she hadn't done a good enough job.

"Sophie, I'm not mad at you." He pulled her into his arms. "I'm fuming at my jerk of a brother."

She sniffled into his shirt. "Well, that makes two of us."

"You don't have to be here. Take the day to relax or...I don't know. Throw darts at a picture of Jake."

She chuckled despite how she felt. "The thought of blowing up a photo and placing a giant bull's-eye on it sounds like a plan. Maybe I'll call Kathy to come over and play with me."

"Well, if it's gonna be a party. You can count me in." Dave kissed the top of her head.

"You just want to see Kathy."

"Maybe."

She pulled away just as Jake strolled into the bar area.

"Hey," Jake said with caution.

Dave ignored him by looking back down at his clipboard, his face a tense expression of mean.

"Guess no one's talking to me."

Sophie skirted away with not so much as a glance. She went straight into her office and closed the door with a satisfying slam.

A low knock sounded on it two hours later. Sophie hesitated answering it.

"It's Dave."

Opening the door, she sighed in relief. "You're not talking to him either, eh?"

"For now. But there's something I wanted to talk to you about." He walked in and sat on the couch. Her and Jake's couch. He patted the cushion next to him. "Sit."

"No thanks."

"Sit, please."

She sat wondering if it was dreaded news, for Dave looked grief stricken. "Jake's hurtin'. And while we have a right to be mad at him, a right not to talk to him, I'm going to ask you to be civil. We have a business to run, and we can't give him the silent treatment forever."

"You agree with him breaking up with me?" Astonishment and fury slammed into her at his betrayal. Dave had no right defending Jake, even if it was his brother.

"No, no, no. I just…" He took a deep breath. "Sophie, you love Jake, right?"

She didn't say anything. Just looked down at her exceptionally white sneakers, not knowing what to say.

Dave continued, "I know you do. What you need to understand is Jake's complicated."

"I hadn't noticed."

"He can be great one day and not the next. Although his mood swings have evened out in the past year, sometimes you can't tell where he's comin' from or where he's goin'."

"Yeah, I'd say."

"Sophie." He took her hands in his. "Ignore him when he calls. Hell, throw darts at his picture. But we have a responsibility to the Hungry Lion, and being the owner, I can't have this breakup affect business."

She gave him a weak smile. "I understand."

"Don't give up on him, Sophie. If you love him, truly love him, you'll see the suffering he's putting himself through."

"But you're also not talking to him," Sophie whined.

"I am out there because I have to be professional. On a personal level, I need to be calm before I say anything I'll regret. He won't be coming over for beer anytime soon."

"You want me to forget about him breaking up with me? Is that it?"

"What I'm asking is for you to look at what happened through his eyes. I'm not making an excuse. If I agreed with what he did, I wouldn't be giving him the silent treatment. Jake was a disaster last night, Sophie."

She folded her arms across her chest with a huff. "Good."

"I thought he was gonna demolish my house. Instead, he chose to attack me."

"Oh, God!"

In frustration, Dave pulled his hands through his hair, a motion Sophie had seen Jake do numerous times. "No, not like that. He was on a 'poor me' trip, and he pushed me into an argument. Jake only does that when he's really pissed at himself. He told me that he wants a family, he wants you. I think he just doesn't know what to do with the emotions he's now feelin'. By stepping away from you, maybe he thought it would help take some pressure off him."

She seethed at the fact Dave made sense. "He said he needed to get to know himself before he could have a relationship."

Dave frowned. "Under normal circumstances I'd say that's a line of bull—"

"But we're talking about Jake."

"Exactly."

They sat in silence while Sophie replayed the scene in her head. "Maybe you're right. And I'll try to be professional—for the sake of the Lion. But outside of work…" She scoffed. Her heart was too damaged to even think about seeing him for any other reason.

"You're the best thing that ever happened to him. He loves you. Don't let the hurt get in the way of forever. He needs our silent treatment and understanding."

"Gosh, Dave. You almost sound like a romantic."

"Don't tell anybody, but I am." He patted her knee and stood.

"He really hurt me."

"Yeah."

"I'll try to keep an open mind, but I'm not promising anything."

"I'm not asking you to."

Sophie stared down at her hands and thought of her hollow heart and empty life without Jake. It was all very depressing.

Chapter 18

Sophie reminded herself *lonesome* wasn't in her vocabulary, even though that was exactly what she felt. Sure, they tried to keep it friendly. Yes, things were very uncomfortable. But then Jake stopped coming to work. And despite her rage, she wanted to call and find out if he needed anything or if he experienced another episode and possibly wanted to talk. Thoughts of him haunted her. But in the end, Sophie convinced herself not to call. Jake felt they both needed time and a break from the relationship they supposedly were having. He made it clear she was no longer in his life.

However, Sophie did find truth in what he said about them needing to discover who they were. It galled her to admit Jake might be right.

With graceful feet, Sophie soared across the floor. She'd been dancing more and more since the split, and it wasn't a bad thing. Her mind seemed to slowly clear of the clutter. And, for the first time ever, she felt as if she belonged right where she was.

In the weeks since their breakup, Sophie went from fighting every battle her parents threw at her to picking the ones that required her energy—something she became very stingy with. After the fight with Jake, she had been spent for a good week.

Sophie leaped through the air and landed perfectly. The clapping brought her thoughts from Jake to her father, who stood in the doorway.

"Dad."

"Hi, sweetheart. How are you?"

"Good. What brings you here?" She picked up a towel and wiped the sweat from her brow. Her father never came to visit for no reason, and usually her mother was behind it.

"Your mother and I are worried."

She shook her head. "I assure you. I'm fine." Walking over to him, Sophie kissed his cheek.

"You're single, but we don't know why. Didn't Mr. Sanders make you happy?"

It sounded more like a question than a statement. Weary, Sophie said, "Yes, he made me happy."

"You always had a powerful will, Sophie. Lord knows how your mother and I tried to refine you. Nevertheless, you are your own person and have made it very clear you're not comfortable in our social circles." Nathanial looked at his daughter with concern.

"I appreciate everything you've ever done for me, Dad. It's not that I don't like the fancy clothes and tea parties—they're just so...boring." She gave her father a small smile and he laughed.

"I have to agree with you, dear. I've been extremely bored of them for most of my life."

"That's terrible, Dad. Why do you stay?"

"Because I love your mother, and to be with her I have to live her life. She's not the same woman I married, Sophie. I'm hoping you'll understand that."

"But what has she given up for you? It really seems one-sided." She took her father's hand and squeezed. "Mother is not an easy person."

"She loves you more than you will ever understand. And she has a hard time letting go."

Sophie smirked at him and walked away. "Could have fooled me. I'm going upstairs for some water. You coming?"

"She *has* fooled you, Sophie. Please stop walking and talk to me."

She turned to her father. "What is it, Dad?"

"She holds on because she's afraid of letting go."

"Dad, I'm not a gullible child anymore. She's cold, and I've always been a nuisance to her."

"You couldn't be more wrong. Your mother is afraid to let you get too close because then you could hurt her. But if she lets go then she'll lose you, and that will kill her."

"Dad, what is this about?"

"Never repeat what I'm about to tell you. Do you understand?"

The pain in her father's eyes caused a tidal wave of sadness to overwhelmed Sophie. "Dad, has the business gone that bad? Do you need money?"

"No, no, no. I think we should go upstairs," her father said. "I'll need a strong drink."

For the first time, Sophie noticed the envelope her father held. "It's a little early, but okay."

She watched her father sit at the kitchen table. When she poured him two fingers of brandy he placed his hand on the bottle.

"Leave it."

How Sophie wished she could read her father's mind. What would she find? A lonely man pining for a love who had turned cold and calculating? Would she find hope that a man has for the return of the woman he once married? Or was he sick? Maybe her mother was sick. Sophie's stomach turned at the thought. The woman may not be nice, but she was her mother.

"Dad, what is it?"

He slid the manila envelope to her. Leaving his hand on it, he said, "Your mother loves you more than you could possibly comprehend. I hope this helps with the pain. You both have been fighting so much lately. She needs to let you be the woman you are, and you need to be more understanding."

"Dad, she wanted me to go to the ballet with the two of you and Bruce. Then she wanted me to play the good daughter and flirt with your business partner's son. Somehow, I don't think I'm reading that message wrong."

"I thought you were still in love with Bruce, and we both have seen the error of our ways where that is concerned. Sophie, she needs the dominance with you. What your mother hasn't realized is only by giving it up will she have the relationship with you she's always wanted."

He slid his hand from the envelope and nodded for Sophie to open it. The first things that slid out were photos. Sophie smiled at seeing her mother in the hospital holding a tiny child. Antoinette's hair was luscious and long. It suddenly occurred to Sophie she never saw this picture before. She then flipped to the next one. Her father was in it, too. They looked so happy. Beaming, really.

"I've never seen these pictures before. You both look so in love."

"We were. We still are. Just in a different way. Sometimes terrible things happen to people, and that tragedy is dealt with differently...by different people."

Sophie thought about Jake. Yes, she understood what her father was trying to say—she just didn't understand what it had to do with the pictures. She pulled a tiny white booty with pink laces out of the envelope. "I can't believe you don't have these in an album or something. Dad, there must be thirty pictures here."

With each picture she looked at, Sophie noticed her father drank a little more. Then she came to one where the baby was about three months old. The little girl had dark brown hair and a toothless grin at the camera. There was something else. It looked as if they were in a hospital.

"Dad, this isn't me. I didn't have dark hair as a baby."

"No, Sophie. That isn't you." He swigged down more amber liquid before going on. "That's your older sister. She was born five years before you."

Sophie's astonishment thrust her forward in her chair. "What?"

"Your mother and I were so happy. She was such a perfect baby. From the moment she was born she never cried. The doctors and nurses were amazed. She slept through the night after the first week. Then she…" He trailed off, as if he didn't know what to say next.

Sophie looked down at the photo in amazement. She had an older sister. One she never knew existed. Her parents had successfully wiped out her existence, and Sophie was certain these were the only belongings left to prove the little girl once lived.

"Dad." She reached her hand across the table to his. "What happened?"

"She was very sick, Sophie. At two and a half months she started staring into space. It was very frightening. When we brought her to the hospital to run some tests…she suffered a major seizure and never woke up. That picture of her smiling in the waiting room was taken an hour before we lost her."

Tears flowed for the sister Sophie lost and for her parents, who had never known what was coming. She couldn't imagine the heart-wrenching pain of losing a child. She looked down at the photo in her hands. Antoinette was changing the baby while laughing. Sophie had never seen that sparkle in her mother's eyes. There had never been humor and love shown for Sophie, as there was for this infant.

"What was her name?"

Nathanial wiped his eyes. "Angela. She was our angel. Sophie, you need to understand. Your mother is still suffering. Angela was taken from us before we knew what happened. Before we could say good-bye," he told her quietly.

Speechless from the tragedy her parents had been inflicted with, Sophie stared at the photos. Memories of her childhood raced through her mind. Moments of her mother open and laughing, then cold and distant. It all made sense now.

"You were never a replacement for her, Sophie. You were wanted and planned. Your mother and I thought with another child we could mend. She tried, sweetheart." Nathanial reached across the table and took his daughter's hand. "She loves you so much. But your mother can't reach out to you. You need to go to her."

Sophie gave a rueful laugh, "And say what?"

"Find something in common. Have dinner together, be patient. I know it's a lot to ask."

"You have no idea." She rolled her eyes. "I think I need some coffee."

"Sophie, you remind me of your mother." He laughed a little. "I remember when she and I first met. Gosh, she was the most beautiful thing I'd ever seen. She was dancing in *Swan Lake*, and I was captivated."

"I never knew Mom performed in *Swan Lake*."

"Oh my, yes. She wasn't as successful as you. However, it never mattered to her because she loved to dance. I couldn't keep my eyes off of her. We met after her performance and it was—"

"—love at first sight," Sophie finished.

"Yes, it was," Nathanial proclaimed.

"Why'd she quit?"

"After Angela was taken from us...your mother wasn't the same. It seemed as if someone extinguished the blaze within her that set her apart from everyone else. Sophie, the drive that woman had. It was awe-inspiring. There was nothing she couldn't do. She'd light up a room by just walking into it. People noticed her not only because of her beauty, but because she was so approachable, friendly, loving, giving. I love your mother, and I also miss her." He took down his drink with regret. "I don't know if any of this will make a difference, but I had to try. Your mother spent all day yesterday crying in bed. When I tried to console her she told me she felt dead to the world. That she's missed out on so much with you, and now it's too late." Nathanial looked at his daughter pleadingly. "I don't believe it is. Please...give her a call."

Never had Sophie seen her father so stricken. She'd been wrong all these years. Her father wasn't a broken man. He was quite the opposite—the strongest, most loving man she'd ever known. He stayed with her mother because he loved her and understood that without him, she would surely perish.

"Mom and I always got along when we shopped together. Maybe a day in Boston would do us some good." Her father's eyes lit up. "I can't guarantee anything, Dad. She and I have always been at odds."

"Yes. But I believe your mother is willing to open up. She scared me yesterday."

Her father scared? Her mother crying in bed? These were not the people Sophie thought she knew. "Dad?"

"Yes?"

"I love you."

"I love you, too."

When Nathanial reached out his arms, Sophie went into them. They squeezed each other tight as they cried together.

Nothing was going to be the same. Sophie reflected this long after her father's driver took him home. Her mother turned out to be someone she never really knew. Teenage battles with Antoinette, struggles over career paths, being pushed away yet still remaining under her mother's constant, watchful eye—now Sophie could remember and understand with a new perceptive. No, Sophie's and her mother's wounds wouldn't be healed overnight, but at least the mending could now begin.

Sophie picked up the phone with a deep breath of courage. "Hi, Mom. I think it's time you and I went shopping."

* * *

Jake rolled over and off the bed tangled in the sheets. Schnitzel looked at him with disgust. "Sorry, buddy. Didn't mean to disturb you." He scratched his new cat, who purred loudly. "Come on, let's get some breakfast and make plans for the day."

Jake moved into his kitchen with the large cat in tow. "So tell me, Schnitz, you think I should call her? I mean it's only been several lonely weeks of me being a jackass." The cat looked at him with a cocked head and gave a short meow. "No? Humph... Considering that dreaming about her has become a nightly thing, you still don't think so?"

In his weeks of therapy, Jake learned to work on being himself and how to separate the military man inside from the man he was now. He slowly began to discover what he liked and didn't like. He found time to do the things he had been putting off, like unpacking boxes in his cellar. A small task that showed monumental success.

Jake did his best to stay present and not have lapses in time. To go back to living life where his subconscious didn't capture and torture him with no means of escape or rescue—that was a kind of hell he never wanted to experience again. Where you did and said things without any memory of them. It was a frightening thing to wake one morning and not know what day it was. When Jake first returned home he had been missing lots of time. Hours here, days there. Mundane and repetitive tasks put him in a mental turnoff where he lived soulless and robotic.

He poured himself a cup of coffee with a realization—staying in the moment wasn't the constant challenge it used to be. He had learned to mix things up so boredom wouldn't overtake him. He felt lighter, freer, and more himself than he had in years. He wanted to share this with Sophie, but he didn't think she'd talk to him.

He'd seen her at the Hungry Lion only a few times, and she wouldn't laugh, joke, or even look at him. It just wasn't the same. Of course, how could it be? They were no longer together, and Sophie seemed to have moved on. There wasn't any gossip of a new man, but there was talk of her spending a lot of time with her parents. Her mother, actually. Jake wondered what changed between them, since they'd never gotten along before. Had they finally come to some kind of understanding? He couldn't imagine it was Sophie giving in to her mother's demands. His heart ached from knowing it hadn't been something they shared.

The cat gave him a head butt in the leg. "Okay, okay. I'll feed you, then I'm gettin' myself cleaned up."

He was giving Schnitzel some well-needed diet food when the phone rang.

"Jake."

"Hi, Dave."

"What are you doing?"

"Feeding my kid. Wanna say hi to Uncle Dave, Schnitz?" The feline ignored him and kept eating. "I don't think he likes you."

"Your relationship with that obese cat is bordering on weird."

"He's cool, though. What's up?"

"I have to do a few things that came up today. Think you can come and man the bar from five to ten?"

Jake's heart stopped. Anxiety left his palms sweaty and his ears ringing. He pushed it down and decided honesty was best. "Is Sophie going to be there?"

"Yes, Jake. She works here."

"I just…was wondering."

"You going to put your best dress on and apologize?"

A little miffed, Jake told Dave, "Noooo. I wanted to make sure we won't have the same outfit on."

"Smart-aleck," Dave teased.

"So what came up?"

"I have a few interviews for Sophie's position. Although, I'm still hoping I can convince her to stay. Then I have to go to the bank and blah, blah, blah."

"What do you mean Sophie's position?" Panic tightened Jake's throat. How would he be able to get her back if she left? Did he want her back? Jake ignored the voice in his head screaming *Yes!*

"You can ask her about it when you come in tonight."

"I'm asking you."

"Well, little brother, you're not going to get an answer."

"You know, seeing that Sophie's leaving, she should find her own replacement," Jake suggested with disgust.

"Actually, she's got a childhood friend who's a laid-off accountant coming in." Dave laughed, "From the sound of it, Sophie's tryin' to set us up more than replace herself."

"Humph." Schnitzel rubbed against Jake's leg, so he bent to pet him. "Uncle Dave says I have to work today. You gonna to be okay by yourself?" The cat replied with a squeak then went off to lie in the sun.

"Jake?"

"Yeah?"

"You need to get out more. Oh, and one more thing... apologize."

Chapter 19

Oh, he really needed to get out more, and with the woman standing before him. They hadn't exchanged any words or niceties, yet all he thought about was touching her. He felt itchy, antsy, a little territorial toward the other men looking at her, and desperate to hear her voice. Jake was overloaded with emotions, and he was only on the third hour of his five-hour shift.

They both were standing behind the bar when he made the most pathetic move to get her attention.

"Sorry," Jake said as he pressed his body against the back of hers in an attempt to get by.

"Right," she said in an irritated tone.

Jake looked around at the nearly vacant establishment. Trying to keep it friendly and her out there with him, he announced, "I might be able to close up early tonight."

"Whatever."

He closed his eyes and reminded himself that he deserved this torture. "So, I hear you're leavin'."

"It's really none of your business, but I assure you I'm going to fill the position." Her breasts rested on the bar enticingly when she leaned on it to grab an empty drink a customer left. Jake felt his libido roll over on itself with excitement.

"There's no need to get nasty, Sophie." She went to walk away but stopped when Jake said, "I hear you and your mother have been spending a lot of time together."

Sophie spun on her heels. "Really?"

Jake shrugged. "Have to keep up on all the gossip."

"My mother and I have come to an understanding. And it's none of your concern."

"I'm happy for you." Jake took a long look at the woman in front of him. He yearned for her, he missed her. She looked so beautiful. "Have you been sick?"

She narrowed her eyes, "No. Why?"

"You look like you've lost some weight. Not that it looks bad," he added quickly with his hands up. "I just noticed. I mean... umm, you look really good."

"So do you," she murmured. They stared at each other for a few minutes then Sophie turned to look around. "I'm going to miss this place."

"We're going to miss you."

She laughed with an edge of venom. "We? Or you?"

"Take your pick." The wall she built to keep him out appeared taller and thicker than he imagined. Jake wished he knew how to beat it down with skillful words but all he could do was stare at her and say, "My CDs are a mess."

"Really?"

The sparkle in her eyes encouraged him to continue and break the unbearable tension between them. "Yup. Right now Black Veil Brides is sitting next to Daughtry."

To his pleasure a smile crept across her face. "After we broke up I needed something to keep my mind off of things. I started dancing again, and it felt right. I'm going to teach children in low-income areas. A bus will bring them to my studio."

The joy in her eyes showed a happiness that had never appeared before when she talked about her dancing. It helped Jake with the guilt over hurting her. It also gave him an opening for a new conversation.

"That's awesome, Sophie." Wow, he wanted to hold her. Just so the nerves in his body could calm down. It wasn't only the physical attraction that called to him. He missed their conversations, her laughter, and the feel of her in his arms.

"I really can't wait. The kids I've met are great, and they respond to me really well. I have a few that are truly talented. Its sooo exciting," she bubbled.

Jake wondered if she would've opened the studio if they had stayed together. Probably not. It reinforced the fact that he'd been right. They both needed time to mend and find their places. But Jake still couldn't push past the heartbreak, the loneliness, and the urge to throw all logic away and take her in his arms and beg. Somehow, he felt more complete when they were together, than apart.

"What does your mother think about it?" he asked.

He saw her close down. An iron gate locking her features with mistrust. She even spoke carefully, "Well…she's actually helping me."

Jake passed a beer to someone then began to mix a drink for another patron. "So…you both are really getting along. Very cool."

"We've been doing a lot of talking. I guess when she was younger she always wanted to do something like this. I admitted to thinking about it myself and it kinda happened. It's been really good for us. I hope it lasts," she confessed.

Jake reached his hand across the counter and covered hers. "Me too, Sophie."

She snatched her hand away with a hiss. "Don't touch me."

"My God, you're more beautiful than ever." The words came out and he wasn't going to take them back. "All I want to do is hold you, run a hand through your hair, touch your face." The anguish inside him became a sharpened blade twisting in his heart. "Jeez, Sophie, all I think about is how soft your skin is. That lusty laugh that always reaches your eyes. How your body surrenders to my slightest touch. How could I have let you go? What was I thinking?"

"That's what you miss? You're an ass." She took the glass of water in front of her and threw it in his face.

"Shit!" He looked down at his wet shirt. There were snickers from the other end of the bar. "I was right and you know it," he yelled while sprinting after her to the back office.

"This isn't the time or place, Sanders."

Fighting with her brought him a wicked thrill that awakened his whole body. It felt so good that he pushed harder. "We both needed to discover who we were again. It hurt like hell, but it hasn't been a mistake. Look at all we've accomplished."

"Go to hell." She tried slamming the office door in his face, but he was too quick and slapped a hand on it.

"Truthfully. Would you have opened your own dance studio?" The processing in Sophie's mind showed on her face. "Well?"

"Is this your way of trying to get back with me? Get me to say you were right so we can move on and fuck like old times?"

Stunned and a little insulted, Jake yelled, "No!"

"Then what's this about?"

Sophie glared at him with a malice he knew he deserved. What a mess he was in. There were no words to describe the emptiness that had encased his life since her absence. "Isn't there a happy medium we can come to?" he asked, hoping she would say yes but knowing better.

"Jake, get out of my office," she announced curtly. "And stay out."

The hurt in her voice wrapped around Jake as he walked back out front.

Just then the bell over the door rang, letting him know a customer had entered. Jake glanced up to see a tall, dark brunette with subtle curves. Her sharp features were hawklike, but her lips were almost in a pout.

"Can I help you?" Jake called out to the stranger.

She walked to him with nervous steps and her eyes darted around as if looking for someone. "Jake, right?"

"That'd be me. What can I do for you?"

"I'm here to meet Dave. I'm Kathy," she said, extending a hand. "Is Sophie here?"

"So you're the mysterious Kathy. Nice to finally meet you. Sophie's in the back. I just really ticked her off, so be careful."

"*Just* ticked her off?" She gave a sarcastic laugh but refused to look at him. "What do you call what you did to her before?"

The mild look he gave her matched his tone. "You can find her in the back, second door on the left. Would you like something to drink?"

"I'd love something strong to calm my nerves, but I'll take a Coke instead."

"Here you go. On the house." Jake watched her walk to the back. Her steps weren't as graceful as Sophie's. Actually, everything about Kathy seemed to be the opposite. Jake picked up a glass and started drying it while wondering what the two women were talking about. He itched to know if Sophie truly hated his guts or if there might be a chance they could someday be together again.

The bell chimed again, and Dave entered the bar. "Your new love is here!" Jake announced.

"Thank God! I've waited long enough." Dave shook the snow from his jacket. "Started snowing out there like we're havin' a damn blizzard."

"Really?" Jake looked out the window. "It wasn't a minute ago."

"Nope. But this is New England. We just have to wait. It'll be sunny and warm in a minute."

"Wishful thinking, bro. We're in the dead of winter."

"A man can dream and—"

Jake turned to see what stopped his brother from continuing his thought. "Told you she's your type. Has a smart mouth, too."

Dave gave his brother a brief look before walking to Kathy and Sophie. "Kathy, how ya doing?"

"Good."

It looked almost painful watching his brother and Kathy shake hands. She blushed and averted her eyes.

"Did you find a parking space okay?"

"Yes."

"It's snowing something awful out there. Was it snowing when you came in?" Dave asked.

"Yes."

"Do you say anything other than 'yes'?" Dave gave her a crooked smile.

"Yes," she said, turning a darker shade of crimson. "I'm sorry. I just…" She wrung her hands together and shrugged her shoulders.

Sophie stepped up. "I promise, Dave, once you get her talking, she never stops."

"That's so not true," Kathy protested.

"Why don't you take the booth back there?" Dave nodded with his head. "Did Jake get you something to drink?"

"Yes...I mean...he did when I first came in."

Jake watched her walk away. "Hey, Dave. You want me to order some fries or something from the kitchen for you and Kathy to enjoy together?" When he saw Dave's *don't tease me right now* look, he rephrased his question. "Do you want me to order something so it won't seem so much like an interview and more like two friends talking?"

"Yeah. Do the sampler so she can choose. She's not allergic to anything, is she, Sophie?"

"No. Just really bashful, so be kind."

"I'll do my best."

* * *

"He's a goner," Sophie told Jake, as they watched Dave walk over to Kathy.

"Yes, I believe he is. Who'd've thought a man could turn to putty in the mere presence of a woman?" He looked at Sophie as he said it, and she shifted on her feet.

"A man can do the same thing to a woman." She held his glaze but raised her chin. "Especially one who has no idea of how wonderful he is and refuses to apologize for being a jerk."

It was cute to see the heat rise in Jake's cheeks. She missed him more every day. When Kathy came back into her office nerved up, Sophie had tried to tell her not to worry about the interview. But then her friend saw the tension in Sophie's eyes. That short pep talk got Sophie back on the right path. It stopped her from thinking that this part of her life was a dead end and happiness was a detour sign she missed. Jake *was* trying his best to talk to her. Pretty much came out and said how much he missed her. Except all he talked about was her body and that was why she'd been nasty toward him. The wanting in his eyes told Sophie that Kathy was right. He was hurting, too, and he needed to decide what he wanted. It was the most painful thing she'd ever done, waiting for him to come to her. However, it seemed to be the only approach she could take.

"Why does everyone keep saying I need to ask for your forgiveness? I did nothing wrong," he told her.

"Jake?"

"Yeah."

"Shut up." She saw his hesitation. "You're not going to be able to hide much longer from your feelings for me. They're written on your face."

Jake straightened his body with denial, "Who says I'm hiding? I know what it is I want."

"Really?" She leaned an elbow on the bar, rested her chin in her hand and decided a little push in the right direction wouldn't be a bad thing. "So...what do you want? Me?"

He licked his lips. "Yes. But—"

"But not enough to commit? Do you love me?"

When Jake didn't answer Sophie shook her head, turned, and walked away. She couldn't figure out if standing there facing him was worse than not seeing him at all. There appeared to be a tug-of-war tearing her heart apart.

Chapter 20

That girl knows what she's doing." Dave lifted the barbell up as Jake spotted him.

"Really?"

"Kathy's got so many degrees it's frightening. We're totally underpaying her."

Jake thought of how Sophie lived. To her, a paycheck was more for verifying her independence than for providing financial security. He loved that self-sufficient streak about her. "At least the market is bad and it's hard to find a job. Hopefully Kathy will be stuck with us for a while."

"Hope so. I'd hate for another accountant to walk out that door."

Like he let Sophie walk out of his? Jake missed the stolen glances at work and the silent understanding that went between them without his ever having to explain why he needed alone time. "I bet you would," he commented with a grumble.

"Jake, she's an employee, and you know our policy."

"Yup."

"I'm absolutely breaking that rule and dating her. I don't care.

I swear from the moment I met her…" Dave put the barbell down and sat up. "She's the one," he told Jake with conviction.

"Damn, that didn't take long."

"I'm telling you. Sitting in that booth with her was like sitting with someone I'd known all my life. And she felt it, too."

"How can you be so sure about that?"

"Because I told her, and she said she felt the same."

Taken back, Jake gave a low whistle. "Guess you have Sophie to thank for this."

"I called her this morning and did just that. You know, Jake, she's the best thing to ever happen to you."

"I just think we need some time."

"Well, I'm gonna give you some brotherly advice whether you want it or not. I think you're scared."

Jake gave Dave a bland look. "That wasn't advice, Dave."

"You're terrified and don't know what to do."

"First of all, I've never been terrified of a woman—"

"You are of this one," Dave interrupted.

"Am not. And second…" Jake faltered, trying to remember the reasons they weren't and couldn't be together.

"That's what I thought! You have no idea what you're doing. Let me tell you Jake, you're gonna lose her if you don't do something."

"I can't," Jake whispered. "It's humiliating to admit I'm chickenshit. But I just can't bring myself to go to her. What if she rejects me? I'll die. I can't stop thinking about her, though. How she feels in my arms. How when we're together it's…wow."

"No, I was wrong, Jake. You're an asshole. Is sex all that you think about when you think of her? What are you, sixteen years old?"

"That's not fair, bro." Jake pointed at his brother. "There are plenty of things I miss about her."

"Really? Like what?"

"How we laugh watching TV together. How her perfume is still in the air even though she's gone. Ummm...how she feels next to me."

"Great. Totally great, Jake. You can have that with other women. What is it about Sophie that makes you want *her*? Or are you just being pigheaded about this and don't want to admit you're in love with her?"

Jake hesitated, "She's not gonna take me back anyway."

"For argument's sake, let's say 'I'm sorry' comes out of your mouth."

Jake slugged down some water to give himself time to think before answering. "I don't want to screw up her life like I've done to my own, Dave. *Okay?* I got people hurt and killed."

"Jake, you're not going to wreck her life when you never messed up your own. It was a war and you did your job. Get over yourself." Jake twisted with shame when he saw his brother look helpless for a fraction of a moment. "You need to stop thinking like that and try to move on."

"I know," Jake agreed.

"Are you in love with her?"

"Dave, Sophie deserves more than me."

The disgust in Dave's voice was potent. "Yeah, because war heroes are such scum. Yes or no, Jake? Are you in love with her?"

"I'm no hero," Jake insisted while carefully dodging the question.

"Really? Because that's what all those metals stand for."

"I was doing my job."

"Damn it, Jake! Are you in love with her!"

"Yes! I miss the way her eyes light up when she sees me. I miss the way she answers the phone when she knows I'm on the line.

The way she makes me feel alive when I think the whole world is collapsing around me. I'm not missing a part of myself when I'm with her. Do you understand what it's like to feel as if you're only half a man? That's what I am without her. But I'm no hero, and being with me requires her to put her life on hold—like you did! So I've screwed you, too!" Jake couldn't stand to have this argument any longer and walked away. How could he explain to Dave that as a military man he looked at things much differently? He saw the men who died while under his command. He saw the innocent victims who just happened to get caught in the cross-fire. No, he was no one's hero. Not even his own.

"Jake!" Dave caught up with his brother. "Wait! Let me put it this way. When a man does his everyday job right, he gets a promotion and sometimes a raise for the mundane tasks that make up his day-to-day work. When you guys do something right, it means you saved more lives than you lost. That you fought for the greater good and won. And while at the end of the day you may think you didn't do your job the best that you could...it's still a job that ninety percent of us couldn't do. Because we don't have the grit and courage that you men have. So don't stand there and tell me that you're not a hero because it's insulting to those of us who look up to you! If you can't admit to it, at least acknowledge it! She loves you because of who you *are*, not who you were."

Dave stormed off, leaving Jake to wonder if his brother's point was valid. People always looked up to him and what he did. From strangers, to old school friends, to family. They always wanted to know how he could do what he did and be the man he was. The man he used to be. Jake remembered seeing admiration in some of his young cadets' eyes and knew he once looked like that when meeting his own heroes. He mulled over how proud he used to be for what he did for his country. How maybe he had lost that pride with the aftermath and the melee his life turned into. He had once believed in this nation so much that he almost gave his life for it. Given the chance, would he do it again knowing the consequences? The answer came easy: Yes. Without question.

Later that night, Jake laid out his uniform and medals on his bed. They always sat in their cases, which were tucked high on the shelf in his bedroom closet. He couldn't remember the day his last honor was given to him, because it happened at the beginning of his downward spiral. What he could recall, though, was feeling a sense of pride. All the men he looked up to had gotten that medal. Now he had it, too. But what did the shiny symbol mean to him? That he did his job right, and to the best of his capabilities? That he *was* a hero? Or did the honor mean nothing? Jake ran his thumb over it. No, it meant something. Otherwise, he would have to believe all the casualties of war were for nothing. Callahan's and Chuck's deaths would be for nothing.

Hell, Chuck blew his brains out and left family and friends wondering why. Jake knew the *why*. He lived the *why* every day. He never thought dying in that ditch would have been better than living with the emotional death that ensued. But sometimes when he felt overwhelmed by life and it caused him to act irrational, Jake wondered if Chuck had just needed to stop the pain, to bring an end to the countless images burned into his brain and the constant concern in people's eyes. Casualties aren't just the wounded and dead. No. They are the men and women who return home and discover blending back into civilian life is next to impossible without turning off a switch—the one thing Chuck couldn't find once the only thing he knew was gone.

Looking up, Jake found his reflection in the bedroom mirror. Who was he now that he didn't answer to Gunny? What did he want to do with the rest of his life now that he knew he had choices? Disgruntled, Jake put everything back in its place. Tomorrow he would have to call and thank Dave for being so up front about things and sticking by him while he came to his senses. No, Jake hadn't been the easiest person to be around or work with, but Dave did it not only because they were brothers, but because they understood, respected, and loved each other.

Jake didn't want to think about it anymore. It wore on his mind and exhausted his body. Sleep came easily, and so did the sweet dreams of Sophie—the one person who changed everything. She taught him how to appreciate life again with her quiet understanding and take-no-prisoners attitude. He wasn't whole without her, and not because war ripped an abyss of pain through him, but because her mere absence did. He needed to get her back no matter the cost. Begging on his knees until she forgave him or he died of old age was something he was prepared to do if it meant there was a chance at spending eternity with her. Tomorrow. He was putting on his big-boy pants and getting her back tomorrow.

Chapter 21

The frozen trees glistened as crystals would in the sunlight. Car doors stuck and wipers broke when their owners attempted to dislodge them from their arctic resting place. Jake looked outside his window and wondered for the millionth time what Sophie was doing, thinking, planning for this New Year's Eve.

Pacing with a nervousness he only felt before going into battle, Jake scanned his living room shelves and smiled. They were a little disorganized and dusty. His eyes then wandered to the photos hanging on the walls. One of Dave, Sophie, and him at the Halloween party. Another one of his parents smiling, and another of him and Sophie the night they all ate together. Dave had snapped it with his phone when Jake pulled her in his arms for a good-night kiss. He managed to catch the shared look in their eyes. Love. Plain, simple, and in front of him. Jake almost let her go, and if it wasn't for Dave, he probably would have without ever realizing why the rest of his life was so miserable.

Apprehension pulled at him as he pulled on his boots, grabbed his jacket and keys, then headed out the door. In his urgency he slipped on the last house step and ended up on his butt in the icy snow. With his right hip aching, he hobbled to his truck only to discover the door frozen shut.

"Shit!" he proclaim as he pulled on the handle with all his might. Giving up, he banged on the door. "I hate you!"

Limping back into the house, Jake filled a pot with water and set it on the stove to heat. While waiting he put rock salt on the steps so they wouldn't bring him down again. Determined to get to Sophie, Jake walked out the door with the pot of hot water and poured it over his driver's-side door. Steam floated up as the ice melted and the latch let free. With his objective only a few miles down the road he threw the empty pot onto the lawn. With a hardy jerk, Jake turned the key in his ignition. *Click... click...cliccckkk.* He knew he should've gotten gas yesterday. His gas line was probably frozen from being beneath a quarter of a tank and the weather under ten degrees. Now what was he going to do? Jake's head fell with a thump on his steering wheel. The horn gave a week beep.

"Think, Jake, think," he ordered himself. "Dave!"

Realizing he left his cell in the house, Jake pushed out of his vehicle and leaped up the slippery steps. With phone in hand, Jake dialed Sophie instead. If he couldn't see her, then damn it, he was going to talk to her. His hands began to shake as her end rang.

"Hello?"

"I'm going sledding and was wondering if you'd like to come. You'd have to come and get me, though, because my truck won't start," he said in one extended breath.

"Jake, you okay?"

"Yeah...ummm...my truck isn't working."

"Do you have enough gas in it?"

He laughed because she knew. Somehow, someway, she always knew. "No, I don't."

"I—"

"Sophie." He took a deep breath a prepared to confess his love. "Listen, I think—"

"You're thinking? Sorry, I don't mean to be nasty."

"The least you could do is listen before you start tearing me a new—"

"Listen? You want me to listen? You have some nerve, Jacob Mark Sanders!"

She called him by his full name. Hearing her say it with the huff and overexaggerated syllables brought a smile to his face. He did love her. Every damn thing about her and that included her temper. "Sophie." When he noticed she had hung up, Jake looked at the phone and began to laugh. He was head over heels in love with her, and it looked like he was going to have to hike to her place to tell her.

* * *

"How dare he!" Sophie charged down the stairs and into her garage. Her engine revved to life. Hydroplaning onto the street, she skidded before gaining control of the car. They were going to have it out. If Jake thought they fought before, he was in for a huge surprise. He needed to stop toying with her feelings and let her know how he really felt about her so they could move on together or apart. The simple idea of Jake with another woman gave Sophie's temper another reason to hit the gas pedal.

She slid into his driveway as Jake climbed out of his car. Sophie barely missed hitting him.

"What the hell are you doing?" he yelled.

She slammed her car door and stalked over to him. "If you think you're going to take up with some floozy just because I'm not working at the Lion anymore, you're sadly mistaken."

"You're nuts. I don't know what the hell you're talking about." His look of amusement brought on Sophie's thirst for blood. Just before her palm would've made a satisfying connection with his face, Jake caught her hand. "No, I won't do it this way."

"Do what? Tell me there's someone else. That we were just a fling and you're happy now." A flood of tears, held in for too long, began to flow. As hard as she tried to stop her breath from gasping, the hurt she felt from his desertion overwhelmed her. The strong person she'd once been disappeared. As much as she wanted to, she couldn't move away from him. What was she doing? Why was she acting like a madwoman?

"Sophie." His voice became so soft she wondered if she heard it at all.

"I don't know what I'm doing, Jake. You make me crazy." Her knees weakened when a tear escaped the corner of his eye.

"I love you, Sophie. Every crazy thing you do. The way you bicker with me and don't put up with my shit. How you like to sit on the couch watching bad movies with your left leg tucked under you. When you dance it's like seeing an angel fly—it's amazing. I can do anything with you by me and nothing without you. I do love you, Sophie."

She couldn't have heard right. It must be the roaring blood in her head causing this moment of insanity. "What?" Jake wrapped his arm around her waist before she could sink into the snow.

"I was on my way to your house to tell you when I fell down the friggin' stairs. Then the door to my truck was frozen shut. Then the truck wouldn't start. Sophie, I'm not a whole man without you. At first, I didn't know what to do with these feelings that exploded in me when I met you. Now I get it! Love makes you do ridiculous things. We're friends, lovers, you trust me, I trust you, and that's sayin' a lot."

"I—"

He kissed her fiercely, his need strong and urgent. "Please believe me when I say it's you. Only you that I want. That I've been waiting for."

Her head spun with all he was saying. "You hurt me."

"I know. I'm so sorry. Sophie, I'm missing time. And for once I can do something about it. It's you. I lost time with you. I was so scared that I'd hurt you that I never realized how much I was doing that exact thing. I wake up looking forward to talking to you and then remember you're not there. I want to wake up with you by my side every morning. I haven't washed my pillowcase because it smells like you. I miss the way we laugh, the way you challenge me. I'm bored! Oh my God, I'm soooooo bored without you."

"Really?" This was more than she could ever ask for. He was coming to her, but she needed to know: "Why now?"

"Knowing you were leaving the Lion threw me. What if I never saw you again? What if I never got that second chance? Dave asked me why it was you. Out of all the women in the world, why was it you?" He knelt in the icy driveway before her as another tear escaped his eye. "Sophie, hurting you was the worst thing I've ever done. You deserve a man who will stand up and fight for what he believes in. One who will give you that home, children, and a dog—"

"Oh, my God." Her breath escaped her lungs in a rush while her mind went blank. This was the man she'd been waiting for, and he was prepared to give her everything she'd ever dreamed of.

"You make me want to be the man to give it to you. You

humble me and I will beg until the last breath leaves me. I love you. I—"

"—don't have to beg, Jake. I love you, too." She fell to her knees in front of him.

Jake rested his forehead on hers. "Don't ever let me go. I know I can get through this with you by my side. It's a whole new world for me, and I want you to be a part of it. I want to build a family with you and memories. Life will mean nothing without you." He heard Sophie let out a giggle. "What?"

"I'm sorry, Jake. You thought you had a choice in this? I was just giving you time to come to your senses. You're mine, and we're going inside that house and I'm going to show you just what you've been missing."

"Yikes. Should I be scared? This sounds like a battle."

"One you're going to love losing."

Don't miss the next book in the
Unlikely Love Series!

Turn the page for a sneak peek of

Tempting Mr. Perfect.

Chapter 1

She walked out the door without even a good-bye. Dave's heart sank to his feet while his stomach churned and his mind tried to think of any way to make her stay. Never a man to beg, Dave realized that might be exactly what he would have to do in order for Kathy to open her eyes and understand where she belonged—with him. He came around the bar and began closing up the Hungry Lion Bar-n-Grill for the night. Money in the safe, chairs up on the tables, bathrooms empty, all doors locked, lights off. Every night Dave would wonder if this routine would get tiring, and to his surprise it never did. He knew where he wanted to be, and every day he came in here was another dream come true. Except for the fact that the woman he loved walked out after every shift and never went home with him.

The late-night air hung heavy and made a promise for the following day to be humid. Dave sauntered to his an old beat-up truck that he just couldn't part with. The paint had faded, and the body was slightly rusted, but the engine purred with awesome power.

Hearing her laugh, Dave turned to see Kathy still chatting

with the late-night waitress, Sue. They were standing next to Kathy's car engrossed in conversation. Exhilaration pumped blood fast and hard through his stiffened body. His mind split into two different personalities with opposing opinions. One said to walk over there, grab the chick, and kiss her. The other pushed for him to jump in his car and escape as fast as he could—ensuring his dignity. The meddlesome, internal argument came to a halt when Kathy spotted him. He'd been standing there like a fool, with his keys dangling from his fingers, and starting at them. She waved him over with a smile.

God, I'm such a dingbat, Dave scolded himself then dragged his feet to join them.

"Dave," Sue said. "You work too much. We were talkin' 'bout going out 'morrow night for male strip review. Wanna come and perform for us?" she teased.

"Umm...not really my thing, Sue. But, you could always try my brother. Jake seems to like taking his clothes off." He winked at Kathy. From under the streetlight he saw color rush to her cheeks. *Gosh, she's so cute.*

"I might just do that. You think Sophie would mind?"

Kathy gave a sweet little laugh. "See Jake naked? No, I don't think so."

Dave shifted on his feet—awkward and wondering what else he should say. Kathy wrung her hands while Sue kept smiling at them both.

"You know kiddos, I'm gonna run. The husband is waitin' and the curtain climbers will be up in six hours."

Dave nodded. "Okay, Sue. See ya next weekend."

"Bye, Sue."

Together they watched her leave, the last lifeline to easy conversation between the both of them. They stood in the parking lot and stared at each other as if their very next words would determine if the sky would fall in. Nervous tension prickled the air. Hypersensitive hormones made his body aware that the opposite sex stood in front of him and mating was imminent. Dave took a step forward. *Just friggin' kiss her!* They were so close, their bodies brushed, and she didn't back up or try to avoid his touch. He dipped his head so their faces were as close as he'd dreamed about. But, instead of kissing her, he began stroking a hand up and down her arm.

"You should go." His eyes held hers. "It's late."

"You're right."

But she didn't move. No, actually, her lips did in the slightest way, casting a bewitching spell of lust over him so that Dave could neither move nor think. A voice echoed in his head: *Kiss me, Dave. Do it now!* With the world around them diminished, and his self awareness no longer his own, Dave brought his lips to hers. Testing, tasting, and cautious. His eyes closed, heightening his other senses, increasing his anticipation. Hands, gentle and soft, cupped both Dave's checks then glided into his hair. Oh, he felt about to come undone. Soon, there would be no going back to sanity. Not if he didn't loosen the strong hold he had around Kathy's body. The kiss went deeper, and Dave soon found his body pressed between her Prius and her. She hooked one leg on his hip. Dave accepted this gift by grasping her thigh and lowering himself so their intense brazes met and created a fierce inferno. Touching her wasn't enough; he wanted more. He needed more.

Tearing his mouth from hers Dave managed to say, "Come home with me."

Kathy opened her mouth and replied in serious honesty, "*Beep…beep…beep…beep.*"

"Oh, what the hell!" Rolling over in bed, Dave slapped the alarm. "Every time I get the balls to make a move on her, I'm interrupted! Damn it!" He threw the alarm across the room, and it slammed into the wall and fell broken to the floor. Hard and sex deprived, Dave covered his eyes with his arm. "You're pathetic. A pathetic man with a crush on a gorgeous woman who pretends to know you're alive and avoids ya as much as she can."

Showered and testy, Dave headed out. The ground, frozen and slick, welcomed him to slide into his driver's-side mirror. *Nope. Can't be spring and can't be summer. Nope, Dave, you're in the middle of the worst winter in New England history!* He rubbed his elbow fast, to help with the pain, then climbed into his truck. *The day will get better, the sun is shining, the birds are chirping, and the truck is fired up.*

Dave kept these happy thoughts in mind as he scrolled through his radio for something to listen to. Turning right on Main, he made his daily stop at the local convenience store. Another coffee for him, one for Kathy, a paper, and Ring-Dings—the breakfast for future Olympians. The clerk greeted him with gossip and obituary news, then gave a "See you tomorrow, Dave" before moving on to the next customer.

Back on the slick road, the old truck gave a lurch and a belch. Dave didn't pay it much mind, because it was around twenty degrees outside, and the old vehicle tended to get temperamental. He couldn't blame it. The weather sucked outside and—the crash came first, then the jolt, then blackness.

As if waking from a deep dream, Dave's mind told him to move because he felt uncomfortable. However, as he began to shift, he found a restraint across his chest was holding him in place. His body was hanging toward the right. Dave suddenly realized he wasn't in bed.

"Dave! Dave! Oh my Gawd!"

The familiar voice penetrated his hazy mind and forced his eyes to open. A kaleidoscope of color blurred his vision, then the colors slowly melted together to form objects his mind still tried to grasp. "Kathy?" A weak question, even to his own ears.

"Yes. I'm right here."

He turned his head to look up, and through the driver's-side door he saw her. "Jesus. Am I dreaming?"

"I'd say it's a nightmare." She reached down and touched his check. "The ambulance is on its way."

"Never a nightmare if you're in it." His head became too heavy to hold up. "I think I'm gonna vomit." Just as the words finished coming out, breakfast and coffee followed. The sound of the sirens only made it worse as he reached for the belt that pinned him in place. "I need a napkin and to get the hell outta here."

"No." That one forceful word stopped him.

"I'm hanging in my truck Kathy, and I just upchucked on myself."

"You may have some serious injuries from the jerk that ran the red. And I can guarantee a concussion. Rolling a spin and a half will do that. Just hang there a little longer." She gave a small chuckle. "No pun intended."

"I love you, Kathy. Always tryin' to get a laugh outta everyone." Dave closed his eyes. He could hear the emergency men asking Kathy to step back, then more glass breaking and a man talking.

"Hey buddy. How's it hanging?"

"Not very comfortably right now," Dave said, smirking. "You wanna watch your step. I lost my stomach in here."

"I've seen worse." The man supported Dave's neck with a brace, then supported Dave's body with his own. When the seat belt was opened, the man slowly lowered Dave. "What's your name?"

"Dave."

"That pretty lady out there your woman?" As his rescuer talked, he and another man, who Dave assumed was his partner, pulled him out of the mangled truck.

"Future wife if I can ever get her to notice me," Dave replied.

"Well, I don't think that's a problem now." An icy stethoscope moved around Dave's chest. "Hurt anywhere?"

"My back."

"Move your toes…good. Fingers…good. Now look at the light…follow it…good. Okay, Dave, you're gonna be takin' a trip to the hospital. There's room service and nurses—"

"I'm fine." At the sound of a female huff beside him, Dave opened his eyes. "Hi, babe."

"Don't you 'babe' me. You think you have a choice? You think you're not going to the hospital? You think—"

He reached a hand out to Kathy. "I'm gonna go. But really, I'm fine. A bump on the head and…and…a—"

Blackness.

* * *

Kathy's body had begun to shake the moment she saw the car heading for Dave's truck. Her heart lurched forward in her chest as the inevitable happened before her. Terror streaked through her psyche as she watched his truck roll over then come to rest against a tree. Kathy jerked her car off the road, slammed on her brakes, and sprinted toward the wreckage—and Dave.

"Please don't be dead. Please be okay." Kathy had repeated the chant again and again, in hopes the words would make it true.

With a jump stronger than she ever thought possible, she had leaped atop the overturned truck to look down and in the driver's-side window. His body had just been hanging there. No movement, no sounds. She'd reached out to touch him while her mind reeled with the memories of the man who dangled quietly in all the chaos around them.

On her first day of work, Dave brought her flowers. Feeling enchanted by him and the blossoms, she kissed his cheek—a daring move for a woman who preferred solitude. Growing up with parents as outgoing as her own made being the center of someone's attention an uncomfortable place to be. And the consideration he gave her every day after that, the little gestures like coffee and bagels every morning, started her thinking that maybe he wasn't the wild man she first thought she was attracted to. Not that having a really nice guy notice you wasn't a great thing, but she had wanted that spark, that danger, the bad guy doing the right thing. As far as Kathy could tell, Dave didn't have a rebellious bone in his body, and she was doomed to live a life as dull as herself. The miserable truth was that it seemed no man had that fundamental component.

Immediately that thought brought a sense of sadness as Kathy fidgeted with her phone in the hospital waiting room. She knew that Angry Birds really wasn't the game to play if she wanted to keep herself calm.

"Kathy! What the hell happened?" Jake, Dave's younger brother, stormed into the waiting room. "Where is he?"

She stood slowly and gave her best friend—Sophie, who was Jake's girlfriend—a hug. "It was awful!" Tears she'd held back spilled down her face. "I saw the guy coming. Dave pulled out in front of me at the light and..." Her throat burned as she related the nightmare. Their faces distorted from shock and concern only made her more upset.

Stomping away and back again, Jake asked, "What about the asshole who hit him?"

Kathy shook her head. "I don't know. He seemed really drunk as he climbed out of his passenger's-side window—his driver's side was smashed. Then he stumbled over to Dave's truck and started yelling at him, me, and the EMTs."

"Jerk," Sophie said.

Kathy could feel her breath quickening while her soft, quiet voice pitched higher. "There was so much blood on that jerk's face and he didn't even know it. How could a person not know they're bleeding like that? I mean...it was everywhere."

"Sit down, Kathy." Sophie took her by the shoulders and directed her to sit in a chair. "Have the doctors come in and told you anything?"

"They're observing him right now. He definitely has a concussion and maybe a broken arm."

"I'll be back."

Kathy and Sophie watched Jake bolt out of the room. Never known for being a calm man, they could hear him demanding the receptionist to get him information on Dave. With a little giggle, Sophie turned back to Kathy.

"Isn't he the best?"

"He's probably intimidating the heck out of that poor woman."

"Naw. He's all bark." Sophie eyed Kathy, almost as if searching for something she hadn't yet told her.

"What?"

"Are you okay? I know if I saw something like that happen to Jake, I'd freak out."

"I'm all right. Just shaken, is all." *That's an understatement*, Kathy thought while looking down at her unsteady hands.

They sat quietly for what seemed like forever. People rushed in, people rushed out. Every time a doctor would poke his or her head in, every waiting body would jolt to attention. The purgatory became nerve-racking—to get so hopeful and then find the physician was there for someone else.

Jake finally returned to the waiting room. "Bad concussion. Whiplash, sprained arm, and lucky to have been wearing his seat belt," he informed them.

The women each let out a long breath.

"He's staying the night, and we'll be able to see him in a few." Jake's lips twisted in disgust. "In hospital time, I think that means one hour."

"Probably," Sophie said.

About the Author

Once Rebecca Rose picked up her first romance novel she knew her destiny was typed on those pages. She lives to find romance in ordinary life doing everyday things, and believes we need only to be mindful enough to find it. While being slightly dyslexic creates some challenges, she feels compelled to write about the characters who reside in her head.

Now with multiple books published, she is a full-time writer with a nag for a muse who talks obsessively, even in the car. That is, of course, when the voice can get a word in edgewise with her three children and husband of nineteen years along for the adventure.

Rebecca hopes her writing brings you to laugh, cry, and rejoice with her characters. Maybe even leave a lasting impression on your soul.

www.ingramcontent.com/pod-product-compliance
Ingram Content Group UK Ltd.
Pitfield, Milton Keynes, MK11 3LW, UK
UKHW022257280225
455674UK00001B/60

9 781455 581429